SCHEHEREZADE'S BE

PRESENTS

AS YOU WISH
THE LOATHLY LADY ISSUE

Scheherezade's Bequest Volume 1, Issue 1
As You Wish: The Loathly Lady Issue
Edited by Donna Quattrone & Virginia M. Mohlere

Published by Papaveria Press
An Imprint of Circle Six
France

ISBN 978 1 907881 34 3 (Paperback)
ISBN 978 1 907881 36 7 (Digital)

With special thanks to Jane Yolen for allowing us to reprint "Fat Is Not A Fairy Tale," which was first published in *Such A Pretty Face*, 2000.

CONTENTS

As You Wish:
The Loathly Lady Issue
An Introduction
Donna Quattrone

IT IS NOT SURPRISING THAT FAIRY TALES AND FOLKTALES are also referred to as "wonder" tales.

If you think about the things that inspire us to exclaim, "that is wonderful," they often entail something that we discover randomly or unexpectedly, something that turns out to be a beautiful surprise or a memorable "wow" moment. We wonder about things because they captivate our senses or ignite our imagination. Wonder is the spark that jolts us out of complacency; it prompts an awareness of something "other," something more, it hints at myriad possibilities. Wonder, then, has the remarkable capacity to encourage a different way of viewing the world; it tosses us outside the box of normal perception, it leads us above and beyond the mundane and into the marvelous. It can, if we let it, foster transformation. And it is exactly this kind of exploratory dance of wonder that is paramount in the tale of the Loathly Lady.

Throughout oral and written history, the Loathly Lady has had multiple incarnations. It's likely that many of you know her from Chaucer's "Wife of Bath's Tale," which is framed around the question of "What is it that women really want?" The narrative challenges societal expectations of beauty and also addresses notions of equality, autonomy, perception and love. As all of these issues are equally relevant today, it is no wonder that the Loathly Lady's tale endures.

I think one of the things I like best about the Loathly Lady archetype is that it employs a sense of wonder in a manner that is not always epitomized in fairy tales. It serves to invert the "princess as heroine" paradigm; instead it is the unlikely helper that is moved from the shadows to the center of the stage and, from there, it is she who prompts a truly wondrous discovery. In a feat that is no small magic, the tales encourage us to move beyond the viewpoint of that which is only "skin deep" and to consider both ourselves and others, not just in light of that which is desirable on the surface, but also with regard to the personal qualities that reflect true heart's desire. Beauty, then, is not dependent on image, and heroism is signified by respect, love, and the recognition of sovereignty.

The concept of sovereignty is of primary importance in Loathly Lady tales. Throughout the years, the implied meaning of sovereignty has shape-shifted; in the past it has suggested the necessity of allegiance to a deity or of loyalty to a ruler. As time went on, it has often been used to denote self-dominion or personal mastery. In the end, it turns out that what our heroine desires most is autonomy, and the appreciation of such as well. The non-fiction articles in this issue further explore the idea of sovereignty and the way it is utilized in a variety of tales that showcase or are influenced by the Loathly Lady.

The stories and poems contained herein, like many of the characters that people them, are much more than they appear to be on the surface. Together, they comprise a parade of Loathly Ladies, clothed in fashions both contemporary and classic. Despite their wildly varied appearance, all of them resound with deep magic, and are replete with rich and remarkable delights. They celebrate beauty in the strange, the unusual, and the unconventional, and they stand as advocates for choice and acceptance. Along with their stories, we asked our authors to include a few paragraphs about why they were attracted to this particular tale-type, and their responses make for equally interesting reading.

The title of this volume was gleaned from a modern source: In *The Princess Bride*, Dread Pirate Roberts' oft-repeated words to his dear Buttercup perfectly embody the idea of sovereignty. The themes in the Loathly Lady's tale are indeed timeless, and it has been a great pleasure to revisit them here. I believe our authors have done a brilliant job of taking them to new and exciting places, places where prescribed ideals regarding image are re-imagined, where individuality is revered, and where happily-ever-after is as unique as the souls that are brave enough to seek it out. I suspect the famous old crone would approve, and it is in the spirit of The Loathly Lady that I present these tales of transformation to you. I hope you find them as wonderful as I do!

Donna Quattrone

DONNA QUATTRONE is a native of Bucks County, PA, where she plays with pencils and paint, wood things and words. She was awarded a Master's degree in Medieval Studies from the University of Pennsylvania, and is fairly certain that she spotted the Loathly Lady on campus a number of times during her studies there. In addition to being an editor, she is an author whose published fiction and poetry can be found both online and in print. She is also a photographer and a tribal fusion bellydancer and, when not busy wordsmithing, shutter-clicking or dancing barefoot, she can be found drinking tea, collecting black boots and indulging in dark chocolate.

Sovereignty, Agency and Perceptions of the Grotesque in Two Medieval Interpretations of the Loathly Lady

Anita Harris Satkunananthan, PhD

THE LOATHLY LADY'S EYES FIX ON THE ONLOOKER, CHALLENGING perceptions by standing for both female and beast, beautiful and ugly, male and female. As an archetype in folklore and fairytales, the Loathly Lady beguiles not with physical beauty, but with the power of transformation, and that of choice. I read the Loathly Lady as a liminal, inherently hybrid being, and examine the significance of the element of the grotesque in her appearance. I am interested in the manner in which the perception of beauty and of the grotesque connects to cultural expectations of beauty, but these expectations also shift with the times. In this article, I refer to the depictions of both Dame Ragnelle in *The Wedding of Sir Gawain and Dame Ragnelle* and that of the Loathly Lady in the *Wife of Bath's Tale*. Much has been written concerning the cultural, psychological and social significances of both accounts by medieval scholars. Following from this, I look at sovereignty and the implications of that choice from a gendered perspective, taking into account agency and the manner in which the Loathly Lady, while standing in seemingly as an agent of civilisation (ergo, ensuring that her husband meets the specifications of a virtuous mate), is really at odds with prescribed norms.

In both tales, beauty is only one part of the paradigm that also looks at both societal and gender roles—choice is an important aspect of this magical transformation. Margaret Schlauch observes that the "happy solution" in all versions of the Loathly Lady, "rests on the deference to the lady's wishes" (417). But what is the problem that requires a solution and what is the nature of this choice? It is no mere gender reversal of the Animal Bridegroom trope. The transformation in the Loathly Lady tale-type requires something far more complex since it is not predicated on love, but rather, on agency and sovereignty, which, in the medieval texts studied may be read as not merely related to freedom or agency, but as a desire to rule, to gain control and power. It is a desire that seems couched in patriarchal terms, which is no surprise, considering the age, but it is a nuanced desire which does take into account the wishes of women. It is entirely possible that a personal desire for agency and for autonomy is read by the male poets as being related to power, influence or the desire to rule.

I read the interpretation of sovereignty in the two medieval texts as an interesting inversion of the earlier Loathly Lady motifs found in tales such as the Irish *Niall of the Nine Hostages*[1], in which the young Niall, before becoming High King of Tara, is the only one amongst his brothers brave enough to kiss the Loathly Lady guarding the well. She then reveals herself to be a beautiful maiden who embodies the "Sovereignty of Erin". The motif of the Loathly Lady has existed for far longer than the medieval iterations examined in this article. This variant reveals the mythical significance of the Loathly Lady. In this earlier form she embodies the longed-for sovereignty in the medieval variants of the tale. Ananda K. Coomarasamy has questioned the significance of this marriage between Gawain and the Loathly Lady, drawing parallels between it and the union between the Sun-God and the Earth-Mother. He writes:

> The tale of the Loathly Lady occurs in several Irish contexts, amongst which that of the Five Sons of Eochaidh related in the Temair Breg and Echtra mac Echdach Mugmedoin may be regarded as typical. The five brothers in turn go to

---

1   Many other variants exist of the Loathly Lady's tale. Coomarasamy has mentioned variants in the *Rig Veda*, for instance. Apart from the Arthurian version of the tale, there are Germanic versions, such as in Wolfram von Eschenbach's *Parzival*. She has appeared more than ones in tales related to the quest of the Holy Grail. There are parallels between the two tales—the quest for the Holy Grail requires that the questor to ask the right questions, and correct phrasing is essential with the Loathly Lady too.

a fountain to obtain a drink of its 'water of virtues,' but it is guarded by a most hideous hag who demands a kiss as the price of a drink. (392)

This is the story of *Niall of the Nine Hostages*, who was apparently so prolific that genetic research has revealed that possibly one in twelve Irish men are descended from this High King of Tara[2]. This illustrious hero displayed no hesitation in moving forward to embrace the loathsome lady, ignoring her appearance. His action is both moving and symbolic:

Only the youngest brother, Niall who, like many another hero, has been reared in exile, throws his arms about her 'as if she were forever his wife'; thereupon she becomes a beautiful maiden and foretells Niall's rule in Tara. 'As at first thou hast seen me ugly,' she says, 'but in the end beautiful, even so is royal rule. Without battles it may not be won, but in the end, to anyone, it is comely and handsome.' (392)

There is a definite supernatural and mythical significance in the union between the Loathly Lady and her hero of choice in these Irish myths. Water is a powerful motif, granting wisdom, clarity and illumination. It is evident that in embracing and kissing the Loathly Lady, Niall gains kingship—and therefore "sovereignty", that ever-present element in the Loathly Lady tale, is bestowed upon the male. Coomarasamy continues:

Similarly, in the story of Lughaid Laighe, only he who dares and consents to sleep with the Loathly Lady is the destined king; asked who she is, she says that High Kings sleep with her, and that she is 'the kingship of Alba and Eriu.'(392)

---

2   *The New Scientist* reported in 2006 the genetic evidence that this fifth century "warlord" could have been the ancestor for "[up] to three million men around the world" (para. 1).

This is an important element that may not be found in either Chaucer's version nor in *The Wedding of Sir Gawain and Dame Ragnelle*, but both ironic medieval renditions of the Loathly Lady have given us the dialectic of sovereignty, as something a woman aspires towards, rather than something that is bestowed upon the man who kisses her, embraces her, or marries her. Sovereignty in this respect may be read as agency, the freedom to decide for oneself, although Dame Ragnelle's version is far bolder in its aspirations towards power. Rather, what the husband gains in return is redemption or salvation by acknowledging her right to choose. It is an interesting shift in gender dynamics, but the earthy and supernatural elements are still present in the Loathly Lady, as may be observed in the mishmash of human/animal attributes found in her form.

It is axiomatic that the appearance of Dame Ragnelle and the Loathly Lady in both medieval iterations of the tale are in the form of a social commentary. This may be read in her beastly, comically grotesque form, aimed at horrifying her would-be bridegroom out of his knightly wits. The element of the grotesque may be connected to hybridity, both from a gendered point of view, and from the perspective of the wilderness/civilisation dialectic. Albeit viewed as a creature of the woods and of nature, the Loathly Lady is still a very powerful civilising force in all of the tales, turning knights into husbands and providing cues on the right way to treat a woman. There is a very strong element of gender performativity in the figure of Dame Ragnelle. She oversteps her boundaries as a gentlewoman, even if we are made aware that this is because of a "curse" that has been placed upon her, making her hideous to behold. The "curse" of ugliness gives her the freedom not to be just a lady, but to straddle prescribed gender roles.

The grotesque is discussed in this article in relation to the construction of sovereignty and in relation to agency. The grotesque may be read in both variants as a projection of the fears of old age. The "Loathly Lady" after all, translates into "The Hag" in some versions of this tale, and the curse that is placed upon a beautiful maiden is that of premature old age, coupled with several other unlovely attributes. The

"Loathly" configurations were not necessarily grotesque in the earlier variants of the tale, but were definitely drawn out to comical excess in *The Wedding of Sir Gawain and Dame Ragnelle*, which serves to highlight the manner in which Dame Ragnelle, the Loathly Lady, may have appeared transgressive to a medieval court. Transgression often implies going against the norms, sometimes by actively breaking the law, but often, one may be transgressive just by being different, or by being hybrid—a composite of more than one element, as may be seen in the detailed description of Dame Ragnelle in the medieval poem.

Scholars have commented on the connections between *The Wedding of Sir Gawain and Dame Ragnelle* and *The Wife of Bath's Tale*. Rebecca A. Davis, for example, argues that the poet of Dame Ragnelle very clearly was referring to not just the Loathly Lady in Chaucer's tale, but to the characteristics of Alisoun, the Wife of Bath herself (430). Davis writes:

> An audience familiar with Chaucer's version of the tale would be delighted by the narrator's account of the wedding feast that follows Ragnell's triumph over Guinevere's attempt to hinder her 'I woll.' Ragnell's loathly splendour '[i]n myddys of alle the rowte' (WSF, 580) produces a spectacle of sartorial incongruity, as all her rich apparel can do nothing to diminish the foulness of her form and her fiendish appetite. (435)

In short, the poet of *The Wedding of Sir Gawain and Dame Ragnell* was influenced by the strident polemics of both The Wife of Bath and her version of the Loathly Lady (as a sermonising bride)—and draws out the analogy to comical excess. This does impact the pivotal moment of choice in both analogues.

The choice implicated in this tale is a choice that accords agency to the female, but it is a limited agency. Both options depend, after all, on the desire of the husband; does he prefer a wife who is beautiful and admired, or does he prefer one who is beautiful only for him and thus faithful? The solution of this dilemma is to give his wife the agency to decide for herself—and it is a generous gesture in a patriarchal world. But it is not an unproblematic one. In *The Wedding of Sir Gawain and Dame Ragnelle* for example, it is spelled out very clearly that Sir Gawain's choice was no choice at all, as will be examined in my analysis of both texts.

THE WIFE OF BATH'S TALE

GEOFFREY CHAUCER'S *THE WIFE OF BATH'S TALE* PRECEDES *THE Wedding of Sir Gawain and Dame Ragnelle*, and scholars inclusive of Davis have indicated that the latter was influenced by Chaucer's variant. *The Wife of Bath's Tale* from Geoffrey Chaucer's *The Canterbury Tales* should naturally be read in conjunction with the Wife's Prologue. Alisoun, the Wife of Bath, is a strong female character. Her tale reflects her personality, as a woman who has married five men, and who champions the freedom and autonomy of womenfolk. In her hands, the quest to find "what a woman wants" becomes layered and problematic. Instead of the question being asked by an antagonist knight, as is the case in Dame Ragnelle, we have the question being asked by the Queen, as a manner in which the knight may atone for his misdemeanour.

Aaron Steinberg suggests that this choice in *The Wife of Bath's Tale* is a wish-fulfilment fantasy by Alisoun, noting that to his knowledge, only two previous scholars, Charles A. Owen and Frances G. Townsend, had similarly alluded to the tale as being a projection of Alisoun's desires (187). However, as Douglas J. Wurtele has pointed out, the character of the knight in *The Wife of Bath's Tale* is deeply flawed in two distinct ways. Firstly, by his unmannerly sexual assault of a lady who then disappears into the narrative. And secondly, by daring to comment on his wife's loathsome appearance—this is a break from the norm of this tale, which usually features far more courteous bridegrooms who know not to comment on their wives's unlovely bits (55). Wurtele also notes that *The Wife of Bath's Tale* breaks away from the norm because the Loathly Lady gives the knight his dilemma while still in her loathsome form (55). And it is a far crueller dilemma than found in the earlier iterations, but then again, it is in response to a crueller deed.

Therefore, it is difficult to read this tale as being wholly a wish-fulfilment fantasy of the Wife of Bath, because it seems to be a tale about wresting power, for the sake of educating. And yet, it is entirely possible that Alisoun may project into the retelling a wish that her youngest husband would see her as a ravishing young maiden. Beauty, however, comes with a wicked price in this tale. The choice that the hag gives the knight is to either have a beautiful wife in the daytime who will then cuckold him, or to have a faithful and beautiful wife by night. Wurtele remarks that this has "corrupted the traditional dilemma, which was not morally ambiguous and even, in a way, innocent, into something little short of vicious" (56). As Wurtele correctly identifies, these divergences from the traditional tales lend an air of reality to Chaucer's version. These divergences from the analogue are, after all, instrumental in the reforming of the knight. Chaucer's version of the fairytale is therefore grounded in everyday life and is all the more resonant because of this.

One of the pivotal differences in Chaucer's version is that the knight receives some kind of tutelage and retribution for his deed from women. The manner of his education is reminiscent of medieval courts of love. There is a fair deal of agency as envisioned in Chaucer's vision of King Arthur's court, a world in which women can change destinies and their fates. The Wife of Bath's strong character however, is central to this. Susan Carter observes that Alisoun sees "that maidens are grist for the mill in the chivalric scheme" as "objects with the limited option of either being rescued" or ravished. (334) The Wife of Bath's response is thus "to rewrite the script, allowing the hag to oppress and reeducate the errant knight". (334) It is her voice then, that we read into this retelling of the Loathly Lady, a formidable woman who has outlived four husbands, and her fifth being much younger than herself—her age is alluded to as being analogous with the Loathly Lady's presence in her tale.

Alisoun's personality, and the personality of her narrative, imbues *The Wife of Bath's Tale*. She is, after all, the woman who asserts her right to have five husbands, particularly since she marries them successively and not concurrently, boasting that "Of five housbandes scoleying am

I/Welcome the sixte whan that evere he shal!". (258) Her voice may be discerned in that of the hag who similarly "schools" the knight.

More than one scholar has mentioned that through the Wife of Bath, Chaucer addresses the question of gender roles and restrictions. Carter, for instance, writes that although "Chaucer is not actually endorsing the strident voice he gives to the Wife, he is certainly making play with textuality, with subjectivity, and with the construction of ideas about sexuality". (329) Although Chaucer seems to be, to a certain extent, satirising The Wife of Bath, it is evident that she casts in sharp relief the stereotypical ways in which the clerics and clergymen viewed women in Chaucer's time. Carter further opines that the Loathly Lady "motif central to the Wife's tale... makes it more feasible that the Wife's tale is centrally about liberation from gender role restriction". (329) And certainly, the manner in which Chaucer diverges from other Loathly Lady analogues seems to be in order to question those roles.

One divergence from other analogues that may be found in *The Wife of Bath's Tale* is that the hag is a fairy who changes form in order to test the atoning knight. She is not cursed, and she does not provide the knight with a peek at her hidden beauty. In so doing, Chaucer empowers the Loathly Lady, allowing her to choose her own destiny, and in so doing, transforms him from a churlish knight into a gentleman. The redemption of the knight is an important ingredient in this tale. Joseph P. Roppolo writes:

> Scholars, almost without exception, have treated the story told by the Wife of Bath in *The Canterbury Tales* as merely a fairy tale, an exemplum designed to illustrated the Wife's belief that happiness in marriage can be achieved only if the wife is granted sovereignty. (263)

Roppolo opines that there are possibly two stories being told simultaneously, "two stories which merge in surface detail but which diverge in moral preachment with strongly ironic effect". (263) However, it is not possible to divorce the redemption of the knight from the choice that connects both the Loathly Lady and the knight. It is a two-way relationship, perhaps more obviously so in Dame Ragnelle than in *The Wife of Bath's Tale*, because Dame Ragnelle needs to be released from her curse as much as Sir Gawain needs to release his Sire from a nasty end. In *The Wife of Bath's Tale*, the Loathly Lady is a fairy who chooses to take on an unattractive form to "test" the knight because he needs to learn how to respect women. As Davis observes, the hag is depicted in Chaucer's version as "a shape-shifting fairy who controls her own enchantment to test the knight", adding that this empowerment "befits the Wife of Bath's audacious narrative". (434) This narrative, and Alisoun's character, imbues the tale of courtly redemption, underscoring the medieval understanding of both sovereignty and choice.

There are problematic undertones to this, naturally. The underlying sexual politics may be read as a very limited choice. But the Loathly Lady's role in this tale is to educate, redeem and civilise the initially brutish knight. Roppolo argues that this is the primary reason why Chaucer's version diverges from the analogues. (265) He observes that Chaucer's story does not parallel the analogues closely," and that the extensive changes made by Chaucer had a distinct impact upon the character and motivation of the Knight. (265) The Loathly Lady's supernatural role here is, as with the earlier Celtic versions, to transform the knight, rather than be transformed, as may be observed by her polemical speeches, aimed at schooling her uncouth groom.

The Wedding of Sir Gawain and Dame Ragnelle

The Wedding of Sir Gawain and Dame Ragnelle starts with King Arthur being challenged in the woods by Gromer-Somer Jour who says the King has done him great wrong by giving his lands away to Sir Gawain. Gromer-Somer Jour says that he will slay the King if he does not, in a year, provide the knight with an answer, about what women truly want.

Fyrst thow shalt swere upon my sword broun
To shewe me att thy comyng whate wemen love best in feld and town
And thou shalt mete me here withouten send
Evyn att this day twelfe monethes end; (lines 90-93)

There is a special sort of significance in this Knight in the woods—
he seems as much a part of the woods as is Dame Ragnelle. I find his
presence in this tale intriguing. King Arthur is naturally beset with
woe at this challenge, but fortunately, Dame Ragnelle comes into the
picture. Dame Ragnelle says she is only willing to give up an answer
if King Arthur can promise her Sir Gawain's hand in marriage. Alas
for Poor Gawain, apparently the King did him a grave disservice by
offering him lands! Dame Ragnelle is described as a hideous creature:

Her face was red, her nose snotyd withalle,
Her mowithe wyde, her tethe yalowe overe alle,
With bleryd eyen gretter then a balle.
Her mowithe was nott to lak:
Her tethe hyng overe her lyppes,
Her chekys syde as wemens hippes. (lines 231-236)

There is no ambiguity in the above passage concerning Dame
Ragnelle's looks. Her face is red, snot is falling down from her nose, her
mouth is wide, and her yellow tusk-like teeth are hanging over her lips.
Davis opines that it is almost as though the narrator is delighting in
shocking his audience with an itemising of grotesque attributes (432),
and this is true. The grotesque bear transgressive elements which may
be associated with parody, and parody is rich in this analogue. Davis
further observes that this "mischievous" poet draws his humour from
"excess" (433) as may be abundantly observed in the next few lines:

A lute she bare upon her bak;
Her nek long and therto greatt;
Her here cloteryd on an hepe;

In the sholders she was a yard brode.
Hangyng pappys to be an hors lode,
And lyke a barelle she was made.
And to reherse the fowlnesse of that Lady,
Ther is no tung may telle, securly;
Of lothynesse inowghe she had. (lines 237-245)

Her physical appearance embodies that of the grotesque and the hybrid: her neck is long, her shoulders are broad, her body is like a barrel, and she has that curse of hanging, unshapely breasts. All in all, she seems to be a combination of various unfortunate physical attributes, and some of these physical lineaments suggest middle-to-old age. These attributes are both bestial and human, both masculine and feminine, and most definitely old (and crusty). There is something very earthy about Dame Ragnelle, she carries herself with authority and will brook no refusal. It is no mean feat indeed to be able to convince both King and Knight to take on a rather unusual suit.

Thou must graunt me a knyght to wed:
His name is Sir Gawen.
And suche covenaunt I wolle make the,
Butt thorowe myne answere thy lyf savyd be, (lines 280-283)

Her bold request for Sir Gawain's hand in marriage can also be seen to be quite gloriously unfeminine, as is her answer about what it is women truly want. This is the first of her bargains in this poem. She possesses the power to do so because she has the knowledge that King Arthur seeks, a knowledge that can save his life. She provides the answer, after Sir Gawain manfully submits to the request, agreeing to marry the fearsome creature in order to serve his king:

We desyren of men above alle maner thyng
To have the sovereynté, withoute lesyng,
Of alle, bothe hyghe and lowe (lines 422-424)

In the above passage, Dame Ragnelle says that what women desire of men, above all things, is to have sovereignty, but the sovereignty alluded to by Ragnelle is more than just agency over self. She wants sovereignty over men, and she wants power. Women, according to Ragnelle, want power over all, both high and low. This bold proclamation, combined with Ragnelle's appearance, seems to suggest that such power is against the dictates of courtly society. This is an interesting juxtaposition with *The Wife of Bath's Tale* in which the Queen and her court decide to discipline the knight. Clearly, both tales touch on the sexual politics of the age.

It is interesting to compare both poems with Coomarasamy's reading of the earlier, Celtic versions of the Loathly Lady, in which the Lady bestows sovereignty and kingship upon the man who embraces or kisses her. In those earlier tales, sovereignty is something that is bestowed and not something that is desired by women. I read this as a significant paradigm shift, one that suggests a powerful, primordial basis behind the figure of the Loathly Lady. Even though Dame Ragnelle alludes intertextually to Chaucer's tale, in spirit, it is far closer to the earlier variants in which the Loathly Lady is more of a nature-based being, thus possessing mystical significance. The Wife of Bath's hag, and Dame Ragnelle, are markedly different from one another. It is this strident articulation of desire for power that sets Dame Ragnelle apart, even if, as Davis points out, the entire poem hinges on narratorial parody. (437-438) Despite the elements of parody, however, the earthy significance of Dame Ragnelle cannot be underestimated in this poem.

At its heart, the story of Dame Ragnelle is ironic—it may be about appearances and beauty, but the story really speaks volumes concerning perceptions of power, and agency. It may be that these attributes are considered unfeminine, but I am also particularly interested in the shift between the Celtic fairytales and the medieval variants. It is about those things that are arbitrarily considered feminine and that which is not considered feminine or becoming. The inversion of the choice reveals the complications of agency, which cannot be read separate from the marriage customs of the age. Steinberg writes in his psychoanalytic reading of the poem that the choice that the knight has to make in *The Wedding of Sir Gawain and Dame Ragnelle* contains a "dreamlike air" because the dilemma is proposed by the wife, and "things happen to Gawain", because he does not create this romantic dilemma. (189)

Being part of the patriarchy and the ruling elite, even as a Knight, does provide Gawain with a lion's share of choice—the choice is between having an attractive woman to have sex with or an attractive wife to show off to one's peers. These are both very limited, gendered choices, creating a difficult paradigm for both the husband and the wife. It is a choice that shows us where the power lies. No wonder a woman in such a climate would desire, above all, to have sovereignty! In such a patriarchal domain, a woman's desires may well be to regain control and power. Who else but a brutish and strong Dame Ragnelle could be the spokesperson for such a desire, even if she is a parody of the Wife of Bath?

In both of these options the woman is still an adornment, a function of desire, an adjunct. One might even argue that the only real agency the Loathly Lady has is in trying to ascertain Gawain's nature as a husband. This is a limited choice, and one may argue that the Loathly Lady only had true agency when she was still grotesque. Agency in this tale cannot be read in a straightforward manner.

The Loathly Lady contains not just attributes of femininity but that of masculinity as well, which she wears around her like a shell, or a disguise. The idea of the beautiful bride waiting for the right words, or for the correct choice to be made by her husband from the options that she has laid out for him, is therefore a mixture of both passive and active, she is both empowered and disempowered by this, albeit granted some agency by the deferral of the groom's choice. By allowing *her* to choose whether she wanted to remain beautiful only at night, for the pleasure of her groom, or in the day, so that she would appear beautiful to the community, Sir Gawain breaks the spell, and gets the best of both worlds. Dame Ragnelle is then everything a wife should be in medieval society, but one can't help wondering if there isn't still a cackling wild creature lurking within her, waiting to slip back in-between the cracks of this tale with the onset of natural old age.

Beauty, The Grotesque and Perceptions of the Feminine

The perception of beauty as being both for sensual pleasure and for social utility may be said to be inherently antifeminist, because it removes agency and individuality from a woman, but the tale of the Loathly Lady is more than about the perception of beauty. It is a beguiling tale because it is not just a reverse Beauty and the Beast with a very complex message, not just about beauty that goes beyond appearances, but about the true nature of freedom and autonomy. But, as mentioned earlier, there is a deeper significance to the half-bestial figure of the Loathly Lady. Schlauch observes that there is a "closer affinity of the day-versus-night" ultimatum delivered by the Loathly Lady. She writes:

> A lady who can or must be beautiful at night and ugly by day is closely akin to the heroines (and heroes too) who in fairy tales the world over are obliged to become animals or monsters by day while regaining humanity at night. More-over, the requirement imposed on the hero—that he give precisely the right answer to a crucial question before a spell is broken and happiness assured—has led to comparisons with many other testings of heroes in popular narrative. (417)

While the ending of Dame Ragnelle may be read as a happy ending, it could also be read as a negotiation and of conformation with pre-existing norms for beauty, love, marriage, and a woman's place in society. It is a message that is seemingly at odds with the answer of "sovereignty", but it is important to take into account the fact that both the medieval versions of the tale are layered with irony and social commentary/parody.

How do we define these concepts of love, beauty, agency and sovereignty? For sure they would have different meanings in different time periods. As Davis offers,

Questions of humor in medieval literature are notoriously vexing. It is often difficult for modern readers confidently to determine what was funny to a temporally distant audience. (438)

Temporally distant or otherwise, we can at least discern that both tales abound with humour and irony. The elements of the grotesque, or shocking, or ribald, as present in both variants, enrich the Loathly Lady's story, injecting elements of agency, empowerment and complex sexual politics. For instance, although agency is present in both Dame Ragnelle and the Wife of Bath, at the end of both tales the husband is still rewarded with a beautiful wife. However, one may read the transformation as a change of perception, of a maturing of a man's regard towards the woman he married. It is entirely possible that the alchemy of the change undergone by the wife is that of a maturing of his regard from an expectation of youthful, flawless beauty to a beauty far more aged and complex. Perhaps this is what is wished of Alisoun, the woman who outlived four husbands and has a fifth who is far younger than she is.

The Loathly Lady is a stirring and significant fable about love and beauty that goes beyond appearances. It may be also be read as a tongue-in-cheek fable about proper marital relations. It may even be presented, as in these medieval versions, imbued with a deep irony, but even in this tone, the underlying message about marital love and beauty that goes beyond appearances prevails. The complete atonement of the hag's knight, after all, is in his realisation that to be a good husband, he had to give his wife the right to choose her own destiny, no matter how limited that choice was for both of them. The cynical tone and complexities of medieval society which colour these narratives do not, in my opinion diminish the significance of the tale and of the archetype. The Loathly Lady is still a magical figure, a woman who stands in-between wilderness and civilisation, the mortal and immortal realms. She beckons at us to look beyond the mish-mash of her features to the fertile, earthy, all-encompassing personality that sits within. She bids us observe the wisdom that allows her to look at humanity with unblinkered eyes, to deliver sovereignty, or tutelage, wherever she finds it necessary to do so. She may not always be graceful, in her guise as the loathsome Ogre, but she most certainly is gloriously herself, whether cursed or otherwise.

౨౨

WORKS CITED

Chaucer, Geoffrey. "The Wife of Bath's Tale." *Canterbury Tales. The Norton Anthology of English Literature: The Middle Ages.* Ed. Stephen Greenblatt. 8th ed. New York: Norton, 2006. 256-284.

"The Wedding of Sir Gawain and Dame Ragnell". Camelot Project. Web. March 2013.

"Medieval Irish Warlord Boasts Three Million Descendants". *The New Scientist*, 18 January 2006. Web. March 2013.

Carter, Susan. "Coupling the Beastly Bride and the Hunter Hunted: What Lies behind Chaucer's 'Wife of Bath's Tale'". *The Chaucer Review* 37.4 (2003): 329-345.

Coomarasamy, Ananda K. "On The Loathly Bride." *Speculum* 20.4 (1945): 391-404.

Davis, Rebecca A. "More Evidence for Intertextuality and Humorous Intent in 'The Weddynge of Syr Gawen and Dame Ragnell'". *The Chaucer Review* 35.4 (2001): 430-439.

Roppolo, Joseph P. "The Converted Knight in Chaucer's 'Wife of Bath's Tale'". *College English* 12.5 (1951): 263-269.

Schlauch, Margaret. "The Marital Dilemma in the Wife of Bath's Tale". PMLA 61.2 (1946): 416-430.

Steinberg, Aaron. "The Wife of Bath's Tale and Her Fantasy of Fulfillment". *College English* 26.3 (1964): 187-191/

Wurtele, Douglas J. "Chaucer's Wife of Bath and Her Distorted Arthurian Motifs". *Arthurian Interpretations* 2.1 (1987): 47-61.

ANITA HARRIS SATKUNANANTHAN has been a lecturer at the National University of Malaysia since 2007. She possesses a PhD in Postcolonial Literature from the University of Queensland at St Lucia, Australia. Her research is focused on the postcolonial Gothic in the works of two cosmopolitan writers of third-generation Nigerian origin, Chimamanda Ngozi Adichie and Helen Oyeyemi. Her article, "Textual Transgressions and Consuming the Self in Helen Oyeyemi's and Chimamanda Ngozi Adichie's Fictions," was published in *HECATE: An Interdisciplinary Journal of Women's Liberation* in 2012 [37(2) 2011:41-69].

EVELIGNA OF THE WILDERNESS

Alexandra Fresch

I GO UNCLOTHED. THE TWISTED LIMBS AND TAIL, THE CRUEL AMBER claws, the tiny horn-spikes behind my pointed ears, the dense boar-bristles glittering with brassy scales in spots and swaths like stellar mange—the shock of all this, exposed, hides a human female's unused curves. Makes me merely a monster. The thin, discouraged people of this province lament their missing sheep and wild game, but they do not question one more monster in their lives. I am not a human to be seen, judged, coaxed, absorbed into their cycle of holidays and harvests and lifetimes. I am simply a beast, come in without cause to their tiny villages from a vast, alien world.

But when I cannot find food, or when the guilt of my thefts overtakes me, or when I simply cannot resist the call of humanity, I go into town. Unless I have found a stray coin in the forest, half-buried and mossy with wild age, I must sell something. I walk my castle's crumbling stone, agonizing over each of its few remaining treasures in turn—these last riches of my father, my grandfather, the Reinhorten barony's cursed line. Though I have filed my claws down to impotent, inconspicuous stumps for the visit to town, timeless habit splays my hand until the tendons stand out like cords, until I can touch the sterling silver filigree and gold leaf and luminescent jewels with fingertips instead of claws. Sometimes I cannot choose. That is when I go hungry.

This morning, though, I chose a silver armlet chased with leaping, emerald-eyed stags and set out in my shapeless cloak along the road. The villagers never ask questions of this strange semi-annual visitor, with her hooded face and raspy voice, who sells treasures for less than half their worth. But as I move through the market, buying slabs of cured meat and sacks of flour and salt, I realize that a young man follows me—and that I have not seen him before. His body tells me he works in town, not the fields: thin legs, broad chest and shoulders, sinewy everywhere else. His eyes are large and dark and subtly lit from within, like candles burning behind an oilpaper screen. Black curls fall to the tanned nape of his neck. He wears the coarse clothes of a peasant but the noble, prematurely stern face of a knight, and when I have finished, he draws unabashedly close and offers the use of his mule to carry my goods.

The sun sets and the young man follows me over the flagstones of my threshold. He shrugs off his cape to unload the mule and a long dagger glints at his belt. He sees that I see. Hesitates. I cannot read his tone when he asks: May I take your cloak?

In the ancient library of my castle, whose leather-bound books I will never sell, I have read again and again the great tales of passion. The *Iliad* and the *Odyssey*. *Tristan und Isolde*. *Yvain, le Chevalier au Lion*. *Le Morte d'Arthur*. Even *Don Quixote*, despite itself. Fairy tale after fairy tale after fairy tale. Love and battle intertwined—monster slain, princess claimed, hero ordained, and all brought to fresh life each time their story is retold. Each immortal raised up by the other two. Or love was itself a battle, a tender chivalric combat of sighs, to keep its own radiant thread spooling generation after human generation into the dark, uncertain future.

So I have read, but never known.

The cloak slides from my shoulders and onto the floor. A noise of shock, stifled in his throat. I know what he sees. But then he looks, and it makes me feel small and naked and warm. He draws breath, draws close, draws my eyes into and into his. Will he touch? My soft, hairless underbelly, bare to violence—or lower? Is this fear or desire? I am the beast of the wild barony. I am Eveligna, daughter of Lord Sibratus von Reinhorten. The monster to be overcome, the princess to be wed. But through which self will this man save me?

We embrace, the mule and the goods forgotten in the seconds or hours or years that come. I am pierced. Entered. And it *hurts*, much more—yet somehow less—than I thought it would. But the pain makes me laugh.

I will live forever.

ALEXANDRA FRESCH is a recent graduate from the University of Colorado at Boulder, where she received a B.A. in Creative Writing and in Ecology and Evolutionary Biology. Her primary fields of artistic interest are gender/sexuality, identity politics, and speculative fiction, especially horror and sci-fi. Her work has appeared in *Expanded Horizons, Silverthought Online,* and *Niteblade.* Currently, she is the chief editor and a co-founder of Apparatus Publishing, a multimedia digital publishing start-up that enhances fiction with illustration and sound for tablet publication. She hopes to eventually become a full-time editor, author, creative writing teacher, or some combination of the above.

"I wrote this piece more to explore immortality—both through one's genes and through one's art—than to challenge conventional standards of beauty. Yet in Eveligna's search for immortality, her answer to the original Loathly question ('What do women want?') would sound familiar: The freedom to live as whatever she is. Even if she falls outside of society; even if she doesn't know herself what she is; even if she is multiple conflicting selves at once, as we all are.

Though it wouldn't be easy, she could live as a human. She could crush herself, physically and mentally, into the shape of 'normal' femininity. But while Eveligna does want to find a place in the world, she refuses to blend into the crowd. Furthermore, her role in her own story is undefined, free for her to choose, because she exists in a superposition state of both 'monster' and 'princess.' The ending's ambiguity was intended: Does she take the young man as her slayer or as her lover? Is she the vital conduit through which heroes become heroes—the dragon to his Saint George, the Medusa to his Perseus, the Tiamat to his Marduk? Or is she the future matriarch and baroness who will resurrect her family line, in spite of (or perhaps because of) its hereditary curse? Whichever state she ultimately collapses into, monster or princess, is a state of freedom and power. She was, is, and will remain the central character of her own story. And she reaps the accompanying reward of immortality."

Cut
Martin Rose

Dr. Mason remembers the day he saw the perfect human face.

Erratic pulse. Rapid heart beat. Flushed skin and increasing internal temperature. A bomb rigged to explode. Dr. Mason ticks off each symptom as he feels them and he waits for them to pass and they do not; and she is still there in his waiting room, in high-gloss perfection. She is not a specter, with her perfect skin and eyes like a wagon wheel with an array of colors serving as spokes. He cannot place what country produced her.

"Doctor?"

Unaccented speech, but not American.

He stutters and his blush increases in intensity. Mason equates feelings to internal organs and thus this display is a breach of decorum, unforgivable! He gestures to a seat and passes a hand over his brow to hide his burning face and palms away sweat on his lab coat.

"I apologize for the length of time you've had to wait, it's been unexpectedly busy."

He opens her chart so he does not have to look at her. He shuffles his feet like a politician who forgot his speech and fumbles for words that do not come.

"Of course, Miss—" he pauses as he looks at her name on the chart. "Mrs. Lincoln. I doubt you need to be here."

"Oh?"

He keeps his face buried in the chart. She exists as a force of sound and scent. "You clearly have no need for correction of any kind, and your chart indicates you haven't undergone any kind of surgery. I don't see how I am in any position to help you."

"Read further, Dr. Mason. I do not think you've gotten to the end."

Even her voice is smooth. He turns the page and stops and all his symptoms of fever go into hyper drive and the blush can no longer be confined to his face as it heats up beneath his collar and he bursts out:

"You want it gone! This is a mistake, surely the assistant wrote it down wrong—"

"I want you to alter my face so I can appear more... normalized, doctor. It can't be that hard to understand, can it? You cannot even look me in the eye. How am I to have a life?"

He snaps the folder shut. He looks out the window and sees her reflection in the glass like a transparent overlay across the fields and the blooming azaleas weeping their petals beyond. The curve of a heart-shaped cheek and skin that is not light or dark but somewhere in between. He can almost pick out the ghosts of ancestors who made it so, like Michelangelo's palette mixing drops of color into a single sphere. Is it the Serengeti, the steppes, the Sahara that made that color, is it Ireland, Morocco, Russia?

"I made a mistake," she says, and he hears her pick up her purse and her keys. The consultation is over. "I thought you were skilled enough to help me."

"You want to be rid of your face?"

He traces a finger over the ghost of her reflection in the window and follows it down the line of her face.

"Dr. Mason, have you ever seen a rich man move into a poor area? You know he cannot sustain his mansion long before others are raiding it and tearing it apart, plank by plank. They want that wealth for themselves. They break it apart and then it is no more. Beauty is like that. I had hoped you would help me dismantle it before it costs me everything, before I am empty of anything that matters. Make me into something new. To be loved for what I am. Thank you for your time, doctor."

She opens the door and is gone.

He watches her figure diminish through the window, where he remains long after he should have left. He does not think he will see her again.

⚘

SHE COMES BACK BECAUSE HER HUSBAND WANTS HER TO TRY AGAIN.

"Are you quite sure about your refusal?" she asks him.

He gives her a seat and when she is seated he takes another chair and sets it, back to back, so he faces the opposite wall and will not have to look at her. He talks to the wall and though the arrangement should be awkward it feels intimate; it narrows the world around them to a pinpoint and he feels as if he's a man on a stage. Or perhaps he just hopes and prays that if he stays this way she will not notice how ugly he is in relation to her. And he is not an ugly man.

"You're asking me to take a scalpel to your face while you sleep, and cut you into something ugly. How does your husband feel about this?"

"He hates my beauty as much as I do."

"That's ridiculous. How do I know this is your decision, not his?"

"My beauty is so great, I make the rest of the world ugly around me. I wanted this change long before I knew him."

He concedes her this.

"That's not your fault," he counters. "Convince me, give me a better reason."

"I will pay you. Far more than you've ever been paid for plastic surgery."

"I have no need of money."

"I offer you my body, then."

He lets out a sound between horror and want.

"I would never rob a rich man's house," he whispers. "I have too much appreciation for the architecture."

She laughs a rough, full-bellied laugh and he swears that he must never make her laugh again. It holds more beauty than her face and he thinks this could be a feeling more dangerous than lust. And then he hooks upon the idea that makes him jerk upright in the chair and sit forward in his seat, rubbing his hands, palm to palm.

"Leave your husband."

Now it is her turn to gasp.

"You must be joking."

"I will do what you want under several conditions. And you must be out of options if you've visited me, not once, but twice now. You won't get a better deal."

"You want me to do more than leave my husband?"

"Leave your husband. You must live with me for, ah, physical therapy after the surgery. You won't be able to leave the house. And in return, I'll do the surgery for nothing."

"Seems like a roundabout way of asking me to sleep with you in the long term, doctor."

"I don't want—I mean, I do wan—it's not part of the deal," he blurts out at last. "No sex. You leave him and come with me and after six months, when you're ready, you can go wherever you like with your new face."

There is quiet in the office.

"It's a deal."

She rises and carries the scent of autumn apples with her and he will see no one afterward. He holds his head in his hands and turns thoughts of beauty and its consequences over and over again until he can think of nothing else.

SHE COUNTS FROM TEN AND FALLS SLEEP AND HE PULLS THE ANESTHETIC mask away as her eyes close. He feels safe behind the surgeon's mask where he can be anonymous and she cannot see him blush. He finds her more beautiful in sleep than when awake and he cannot bear to look upon her for long. He touches her on the forehead to sweep her hair aside and plants a chaste kiss beside the curl of her ear. He withdraws and lets her sleep. He does not cut her and he will not lay a hand on her.

HE REMOVES EVERY MIRROR IN THE HOUSE. HE DOES NOT STOP THERE. He takes away the silverware and replaces it with plastic; he swaps the old tube television with a new liquid crystal display so she cannot attempt to pick her reflection out in the glass. He scours every room of the opulent and ostentatious house he bought to make up for his impoverished childhood and so that he could climb his way up the social strata in style. When he is finished, nothing remains that she can see herself in. He comes back to the office to collect her from the operating table and wonders what impression he will make, if people will think him crazy; Mason is determined to save the last beautiful thing before the world dismantles itself in stocks and bad investments and reality television.

✦

He remains by her bedside until she awakens.

She blinks sleep from her eyes and they flutter with excitement, a sensation of hope. Up close, he can see the gentle slope of her eyelids and how they fold just so—a crinkle of skin at the corner of her eyes that if left alone will deepen and multiply with the rich flavor of age.

"Did it work?"

"Oh, it's just awful! You're ugly for sure, now. If you had paid me you'd be getting your money's worth."

She reaches up for her face. Fingers peck at the bandaging he wrapped her in and he slaps her hand away.

"Ah—ah, none of that! When I was a child my parents wouldn't let me open up gifts before Christmas and so you'll have to wait just like the rest of us, hmmm?"

Her eyes narrow, suspicious. It makes her prettier.

"How do I know that you did anything at all? Nothing hurts."

His expression remains stoic. He knows he has a face some have likened to a doll and, like her, he has been gifted with a rare set of genetics; but he has never had his own beauty dwarfed by another's. It's an unusual predicament and he finds he is enjoying being ugly beside her beauty. He finds it... liberating. He cares less about his features, his rampant narcissism, his expensive car or his lavish lifestyle. The trappings of his empty vanity pale in comparison to the simplicity of her beauty and he takes a childish delight in pretending he knows nothing of this elaborate prank he has constructed around her.

"It's not my fault you're not like everybody else," he says loftily. He leaves her with a glass of water and "a pill to alleviate any potential pain" and leaves her alone.

AND LEAVES HER ALONE.

UNTIL FINALLY, AFTER MANY DAYS AND NIGHTS OF HIS BRIEF VISITS TO give her food and to "change the dressings" on her face, she gives in to curiosity about this man who wants nothing from her, and she wanders out and finds him in his room.

He keeps canaries and society finches there and when she cracks open the door, the finch perched on his hand bursts forth in surprised flight. She shrieks and runs back to her room while he cackles and cackles until he cries with laughter.

THERE ARE SMALL MOMENTS OF GREATER BEAUTY THAT PASS BETWEEN them.

He tucks her in at night when she begs him to and he does it as though she is a giant child. She finds excuses to keep him there longer and longer. He waits her out over several evenings until her sense of boundary and propriety snaps. One night, she grabs him by his tie and jerks him to her face and she kisses him slow and deep. The experience is so dizzying he falls backward, but the damage is done. He can't see the wounds her actions leave. He must measure the marks of love, of attraction, in the increasing speed of his heart, the dilation of his pupils.

ꜱ

After a time, they take off the bandages. She knows he is lying about the operation and she asks often to see her own reflection. The six months are almost up and they have not even slept together yet. He remonstrates himself for what he has done and what he cannot bring himself to do. The time for departure arrives with the winter season, and he waits for her to discover his calculated deceit.

He watches her from the second floor with The Nutcracker Suite playing in the background. She gets into her car and checks her reflection in the rear view mirror. He turns away. The car door shuts. Slam! Her steps clatter up the drive and he waits until her knocks blow like rain on the door. He comes down the steps and opens the door and neither of them notices the mistletoe that sways back and forth from above.

ꜱ

"You did nothing. Nothing that you promised me."

"How can I cut you? Why in the world would I hurt something so beautiful as you?"

"Because it's what you agreed to do. To make me ugly!"

"I make people beautiful!"

"It's not good enough, Mason. I want what we agreed to. You love me because I am beautiful, but would you have cared if I had been any other patient of modest appearance, asking to be enhanced?"

"I—"

"You would never have looked twice at me. And you wonder why I want to cast it aside when I cannot trust the lot of you to have an opinion of me that is not linked to my beauty! Oh yes, the great beauty I am, it is monstrous, grotesque! Cut me, Mason."

He swallows.

"I can't."

"Cut me. And I will marry you."

He closes his eyes and thinks that this is like dying, what he feels. The winter wind cannot fix the heat that makes his collar uncomfortable and tight and his head feels like a snow globe being shaken violently enough to make his brains scatter.

"It's my beauty you love," she spits at his feet and curses. "That's all you love, Mason."

And she goes back to her car and leaves.

‰

HE CALLS HER THE NEXT DAY.

"What?" she snaps.

"Your appointment is at 2:30," he whispers.

"Wait... You've agreed to do it?"

"Will you marry me?"

"If you do it, yes."

"Then come at 2:30."

‰

SHE COMES AND HE THINKS IT IS SYMBOLIC THAT SHE DRESSES IN white. He is already in his hospital scrubs and the machines are set up and the anesthetic mixed and ready for her. He is safe behind his mask where the wounds still smart and the scalpel has left its mark where she cannot yet see.

He went under the knife for many reasons and all of them were for her—he could not stand the thought of transcending her and being the beautiful one, and despite her demands, he will find a way to exalt her, even if it means cutting himself instead. Like a star, if a star could diminish its brightness in an effort to make the one beside it brighter.

He has always known beauty is a relative concept, but never has he cared so little for his own, until now. All of his life has been quantified by appearances, keeping up with the joneses. His career hinged on the marketing of style over substance, patients investing in the shallow promise of his good looks. Who would attend an *ugly* plastic surgeon, after all?

When she comes up the steps he takes her hand as if they are from a by-gone era and he a gentleman helping her from a carriage. She inclines her head and he thinks that this is the last time he will experience this beauty, like a bloom soon to be cut and put in a table centerpiece, and from there to fade and wither. The beauty is in the ephemeral nature of it, he supposes. To last only so long, and no longer.

He leads her to the table and they are silent as though this is the wedding ceremony and this act of surgery the consummation itself. She lies on the table and he covers her with a sheet and asks her to count back from ten. She falls into numbness well before then and he regards his instruments with a sorrowful eye.

She wakes up with everything she has ever wanted.

Her face is changed and now the nose is not so straight as it once was, nor are her lips so perfectly formed; her heart shaped cheek has lost its robust form and been made normalized, tragically homogeneous.

He washes his hands in the sink and will not look at her.

"Thank you, Mason," she whispers.

He undoes the strings that keep his mask over his face and it stings when he pulls it away and turns to face her.

"I love you."

Her eyes widen and she catches at his sleeve, makes a fist so he cannot escape. He lets her draw him down to the table beside her where he submits his faculties to become her patient, to be lulled into sleep with the anesthetic of her touch. She presses kisses over his ruined face and he tastes apples and ether on her lips, the heat of fever in his skin and the blood rushing through him. Dr. Mason analyzes his symptoms and reaches a logical diagnosis:

He has never been so happy to be so ugly.

MARTIN ROSE's work appears in *Murky Depths* and *Sein Und Werden* along with contributing reviews to *Shroud*. The short story "Scanner Days, Starry Nights" in *Art From Art* anthology has been picked up for film by Modernist Enterprises. "Dark Horse" appeared in *Fear of the Dark* anthology with Horror Bound Publications, earning an honorable mention from Ellen Datlow's yearly internet list. Forthcoming work "Sap and Blood" to feature in the *Urban Green Man* anthology. Rose's fiction runs the gamut of horror, sci-fi, and fantasy. More details at martinrose.org.

"I wrote 'Cut' in an attempt to invert the mythology—instead of an ugly woman who becomes beautiful, the process moves in the reverse—here, the protagonists only become uglier. In real life, many of us are ordinary or ugly. It is not a spell to be awoken from. The idea of the state of beauty itself being the actual curse intrigued me and would not let go."

WALLEN

A Self Portrait by Brooke Shaden

I have been asked why I don't try to make myself look beautiful in my pictures. My response is always the same: "I do. We just don't see beauty the same way." — Brooke Shaden

THE LADY OF ST. MARK'S PLACE

Brittany Warman

We see her suddenly,
a red flash against the grey subway walls,
hair like a sunset/cherry/lipstick smear,
her smile as wide as a Metrocard.

Her accordion is old, ornate, a bit of a
romantic smirk at the past,
the ripped fabric of her velvet dress
shows a bit of her leg, her lined hands.

I want to give her something but it's
not money she's looking for.
She swoons and plays, singing, swanning,
faux diamonds at her throat like stars.

She's making them uncomfortable, you say,
shivering back down into your coat,
watching for the next train (1 minute.)
She's beautiful.

Her song's words are in a language I don't know,
but meaning cracks through the smoke in the air—
the loneliness of art and magic, the fate
of parallel trains on tracks side by side.

The 6 comes in, you and I step on.
Through the smudged windows, her eyes meet mine, say
"we are the same, you and I,"
and I believe her, know/love/am her.

I open my mouth to call out her name,
our name, in the language I now know,
but the train pulls away
and the shadows again divide us.

BRITTANY WARMAN is a PhD student in English and Folklore at The Ohio State University, where she concentrates on the intersection between literature and folklore, particularly fairy tale retellings. Her creative work has been published by *Jabberwocky Magazine, Cabinet des Fees: Scheherezade's Bequest, inkscrawl, Scareship Magazine*, and others. She can be found online at www.brittanywarman.com

"I encountered the woman described in this poem several years ago but found her so strange and beautiful in her own way that I never forgot her. She remains an enchanting mystery to me. When the call for the 'loathly lady' issue went out, I immediately thought of her and the way that she drew me in even as she made others look away."

The Woman at the Fair With No Face

Jason Lea

My great-grandfather was a funny-looking kid who became a funny-looking man. (Or, at least, I assume he was. He died before I was born so all my information comes from my father.) He had a bird chest and a face that looked like it had been nurtured in a boxing ring—his words, not mine. In the small town where he grew up, the folk used to call him "the ugliest kid in the county."

They never meant to be mean about it. It was more of a nickname than an insult. And, in a small town, any sliver of uniqueness can be a badge of pride. So my great-grandfather would call himself that too—always with a smile—and everyone would think it was OK.

So my funny-looking great-grandfather once went to see the freak show in one of those traveling carnivals. (Or, at least, my father said he did.) The carnival was a big deal apparently and, in his town, it was pretty much the highlight of everyone's summer. Normally it had the same attractions every year—a Ferris wheel, a merry-go-round (one of those classy, two-story kinds,) fried everything on a stick.

However, the freak show—that was new that summer. My great-grandfather had never seen anything like it in all his 15 years. (By the way, I don't condone calling people who are different "freaks"; but times were different, then.) They had the show in this big red and white tent on the main stretch. It was essentially a series of rooms divided by curtains. You walk into one room, see the freak and then, before you go into the next room, you see a painting that teases what the next freak will be.

For example, you walk into the room and see a 600-pound man. You gawk at him for a while. If you're feeling brave, maybe you ask him how he's doing. Maybe he tries to put on a brave face and he tells you he's feeling fat and sassy even though he's got to be dying inside because it's his job to be gawked at by idiot kids who keep asking him stupid questions like "how'd you get so fat?" and "are you hungry?"

Then, once you're bored with the 600-pound man, you turn to the exit and see a painting on an easel of a woman with a mustache and beard and, lest there be any question, it is captioned "the bearded woman."

So you take a moment to wonder how the carnival people are going to fake a bearded woman (because nobody expects veracity from a traveling carnival). You figure it's horse hair attached with spirit gum or a guy with a pair of falsies.

But then you walk through the curtain and you see a woman just like any other. Except she's got facial hair like a Civil War general. And just in case you still think it's a fake, for an extra penny, she'll let you tug on it. (As long as you don't do it too hard. After all, these are real people with real feelings.)

And that's how it went for my great-grandfather. He paid his nickel (apparently, an exorbitant price for the time) and walked slowly from room to room, trying to engage each of the freaks in conversation.

My great-grandfather was a legendary talker, the kind you'd love to have sitting next to you on a train. He'd keep you entertained from Fort Wayne to Boston. He claimed it was a byproduct of being ugly. "Nobody's going to like me for my looks," he'd tell my grandmother, "so they better like me for my personality." His great secret—to hear my grandmother tell it—is that he, within 15 minutes of meeting you, would find out the most interesting thing about you and then stick to that.

But it was a little tricky to do that in a freak show for two reasons. First, there's already a painting out front telling you what you're supposed to find interesting about each performer. My great-grandfather didn't fall for that superficial stuff, though. It might be unusual that a person has a duckbill but what was fascinating about "Mallard Fillmore"— please, God, let that be a self-appointed stage name and not the result of cruel, cruel parents—was his whistling. His elongated lips gave the music a resonance that us normals couldn't match with a trombone.

"You think I'm kidding but that man was the Paul Robeson of whistling," my great-grandfather told my dad.

The bigger problem was the lack of privacy. A good conversation requires some space. It's a lot like dance. It's best with two, possible with three (if everyone knows what they're doing) and a mess by the time you have four or more involved.

So it was difficult to get anywhere with a room full of rubberneckers saying, "Why do you have man and lady parts?"

(The most interesting thing about the hermaphrodite, by the way, is that he/she was a Shakespeare enthusiast and could bring a tear to your eye with a recitation from *King Lear*. It took my great-grandfather more than 45 minutes to find that out. He had to out wait several parties of gawkers and pointers and hecklers to discover that nugget. The hermaphrodite rewarded my great-grandfather's patience by telling him his/her real name. Its stage name was Victor/Victoria or something terrible like that. But when he/she was with friends, he/she went by Ganymede.)

Consequently, my great-grandfather traveled through the tent at a slow pace. By the time he reached the penultimate room, it was almost closing time and he had the place practically to himself because—let's be frank—no one wanted to be in the freak tent at night.

The resident of the second-to-last room was a man with lobster claws for hands and legs that tapered into a pin drop instead of a foot.

"Ectrodactyl," the man repeated to my great-grandfather over and over. "My deformity is called ectrodactyly, which makes me an ectrodactyl."

My great-grandfather couldn't get his tongue around that fine word and kept saying pterodactyl.

At first the man thought he was being mocked and became angry. He called my great-grandfather a cretin, a philistine and a lot of other things you probably learn as a self-defense mechanism when you have lobster claws for hands.

"He said I was a good example of why some animals eat their young," my great-grandfather later recounted. "That's still one of the most fabulous insults I've ever heard. If I wasn't so scared he might try to snap my head off, I might have egged him on a bit more to see what other jewels he had."

Ultimately, the ectrodactyl realized my great-grandfather meant him no harm and he softened toward him. The man—Burton was his name—told my great-grandfather that his greatest regret was that he couldn't play piano.

"My mother was a fantastic pianist," he said. "I would listen to her play the classics—Brahms, Mozart, people like that—for hours. When she was older, she got the shakes and couldn't play anymore. I would have loved to return the favor but—" He lifted his claws and shrugged meekly.

"You know how some people tell you that you can be whatever you want if you try hard enough?" Burton asked.

My great-grandfather nodded.

"That's horse manure. I'll never be a concert pianist or an Olympic sprinter. On my best day, I can't stop people from calling me Lobster Boy."

As a great talker, my great-grandfather had an innate understanding of when to lay out of a conversation and when to jump in. He sensed it was time to jump in.

"What *can* you do?" he said.

The man did not understand the question at first and cocked an eyebrow.

"You say you can't play piano but I'm sure there are some things you can do."

"Sing," Burton replied. "I would sometimes accompany my mother when she played."

"Would you?"

Burton smiled and sat as erectly as he could in his wheelchair. He then closed his eyes, took a deep breath and began singing "Ave Maria."

He had a solid—if unremarkable—tenor but he hit the notes he intended to hit and that's more than many people can do. Great-grandfather listened for the entire song and when it was over he could hear the performers in other rooms join him in their applause.

Great-grandfather thanked Burton for his song and bid him goodbye. The man said he could sing another if my great-grandfather liked, but he declined, saying he would have to get home soon.

The ectrodactyl nodded sadly but didn't beg.

My great-grandfather looked at the final painting and gasped.

It promised The Woman With No Face and the painting showed a horribly scarred visage atop a lovely, feminine body. It wasn't the actual painting that surprised my great-grandfather. (Nothing could surprise him after meeting Ganymede.) It was how she was depicted.

Most of the paintings were cartoons or caricatures—something to make the layperson smile. Burton, for example, was billed as Lobster Boy and shown being dropped into pot of boiling water. ("I despise that painting," Burton told him. And my great-grandfather said he regretted not destroying it as a favor to him.) The 600-pound-man—Marvin—was depicted as sitting atop the world and eating a turkey leg. ("I actually hate turkey," Marvin told a laughing crowd, "but the artist didn't know how to draw a goddamn steak.")

But there was nothing comical about this woman. Her painted eyes looked directly at you and dared you to judge her.

"Young man," Burton said, noticing my great-grandfather's reaction to the painting, "may I offer you a bit of advice?"

Great-grandfather nodded again, sensing this was a time for him to listen.

"Don't try to talk to Mariana," he said. "Look if you must, but don't ask her to sing for you or anything like that. Look and leave."

"Why?" my great-grandfather asked.

"She's new. Relatively," Burton added. "She doesn't like the people coming by as Marvin does or even accept them as Victoria and I do."

"You mean Ganymede?" my great-grandfather said.

Burton raised his eyebrow again, impressed that my great-grandfather had earned Ganymede's trust enough to learn his/her real name.

Burton pondered this new information for a while, emitting a long "hmm" as he thought. He even tapped one of his claws to the side of his head but became self-conscious and stopped when he realized he was doing it.

"Be kind to her," he advised. "If she chooses to talk with you, be even kinder to her than you've been to me."

My great-grandfather nodded and prepared to leave.

"Wait!" Burton shouted and my great-grandfather stopped.

"Don't get too close to her cage either. She... she sometimes gets a bit wild."

My great-grandfather nodded. Then Burton quietly hummed "Ave Maria" as my great-grandfather pulled back the curtain and entered the final room.

At first, my great-grandfather thought this room had less lighting than the others. Than he realized that he had been in the Freak Show almost the entire day and that the sun was no longer bleeding through the tent's white stripes. My great-grandfather peered into the cage and could not initially see its inmate. Then he spotted someone curled in a shadowed corner.

"Hello, Mariana," my great-grandfather whispered.

The body hiding in the corner shifted.

"Who told you my name?" she replied.

When my great-grandfather told this story, he spent a lot of time trying to describe the woman's voice. He juggled words like "sultry" and "menacing" and "autumnal" before throwing his hands up and saying, "You needed to be there. But, believe me, a blind man would have fallen in love with that voice."

"Burton called you Mariana," my great-grandfather said, hoping he hadn't gotten his new friend in trouble. "I thought you might prefer if I used your real name."

The woman stood. Her face was still mostly obscured by the shadows but my great-grandfather could tell she was wearing a beautiful—if a bit dirty—red dress.

"I do," she said.

Great-grandfather said nothing for a while. He suspected this was a time he should lay out and let Mariana lead.

"I assume you want to see my face?" she finally asked.

"I don't have to," he replied.

"No, you paid your nickel"—she chewed that last word like a bit of gristle—"and you deserve your thrill."

She stepped into the light.

My great-grandfather first looked at her body. (He wanted to save her face for last.) She had the figure of a model or a movie star, he told my father. From the neck down, she could have been Jayne Mansfield or Barbara Eden. The people behind the Freak Show understood this and dressed her in what would have been a striking red number if someone had bothered to dry clean it. My great-grandfather also spotted a red high-heel shoe lying in the corner of the cage.

Before he took a glimpse of her face, he asked, "Where is your other shoe?"

"Behind you," Mariana said. "Some people didn't know how to behave so I had to quiet them myself."

My great-grandfather turned, picked up the shoe—its heel had snapped—and gave it to her. This was when he got his first good look at Mariana's face and my great-grandfather needed all of his self-control to stifle his reaction.

What made her horrible wasn't what was missing. No, my great-grandfather had been prepared for that. What unnerved him was what was still there. Two chocolate brown eyes, long black hair and two of the most beautiful lips he had ever seen were attached to a pile of misshapen lumps and scars.

Mariana could tell she had scared the young man so she retreated to her corner.

"Don't," my great-grandfather begged. He used his eyes to apologize and Mariana slowly walked back to the edge of her cage.

My great-grandfather gently reached out and stroked the woman's hair. ("You ever felt alpaca fur?" he asked my dad. "It was that soft.") He then looked her right in those two pools of chocolate and didn't flinch.

"Who did this to you?" he asked.

Mariana sat cross-legged in her cage so she and my great-grandfather were eye to eye. He later admitted to my father that he couldn't help trying to sneak a quick look up her dress.

"Just a boy," she said.

"But why would he?" my great-grandfather asked.

"Some boys get jealous over things that never belonged to them."

My great-grandfather reached for Mariana's hand and she let him take it. "You're beautiful," he told her.

Mariana laughed. It wasn't a pretty laugh either. It's that laugh you hear when the water boy asks the head cheerleader to prom.

"Really?" she said scornfully. "I'm beautiful. Then why don't you give me a kiss?"

She closed her eyes and puckered her lips in a mocking pantomime.

My great-grandfather took a moment too soak in Mariana—all of her, including her misshapen lumps and crisscrossing scars—and decided she wasn't a freak.

My great-grandfather had spent most of his life being called "ugly" or some variant thereof so he probably understood Mariana better than the other nickel-paying gawkers, maybe as well as some of her fellow performers. He figured a person with lobster claws or a duck bill deserved love as much as anyone else. As much as he did.

So he leaned forward and kissed her through the bars.

"That was the best kiss of my life," my great-grandfather told my dad. "It could have powered a light bulb. I could feel her whole life story in that kiss. Without using a single word, she told me about her sadness and her passion and her rage. But you know what I felt? More than any of that? Loneliness."

After a moment—a long moment—Mariana pulled back her head and tilted it quizzically. She then appraised my great-grandfather as he had done her. She must have been satisfied because she asked, "You think I'm beautiful?"

"Yes."

"And you're not teasing me."

"No."

"And you don't think I'm... an oddity?"

"God, no."

Mariana played with a strand of her long, black hair.

"The carnival doesn't move on until Sunday," she said. "Maybe you could visit me again tomorrow?"

My great-grandfather used to claim that poverty was a virtue, using this part of story as evidence. According to him, if he had had another nickel, he would have visited Mariana the next day and maybe this whole tale would have ended differently. But he didn't have a single penny left and he knew he couldn't get more in time, so his poverty made him brave, if a bit desperate.

"Or you could just leave with me now," he said.

Mariana stopped running her hair through her long, elegant fingers. "What?"

"You're not happy here," my great-grandfather said, "and, while I may not be the handsomest man in the county, I promise I'd always be kind to you. And I'd never lay a hand on you, except to touch your cheek."

Mariana smiled without humor. "You'd touch this cheek?" she said, pointing to a lump on the side of her face.

"Come closer," my great-grandfather whispered.

Mariana closed her eyes—which, in hindsight, was a remarkable show of trust on her part—and brought her face between the bars. My great-grandfather gently rested the back of his fingers against where her cheek would have been.

She leaned into the touch like a kitten getting its whiskers scratched.

Then my great-grandfather moved his hand to the back of her head, stroked her long hair and kissed her once more.

Mariana pulled her face away a second time. "OK," she said.

My great-grandfather gave a whoop but Mariana shushed him.

"It might be better if we do this quietly," she said.

My great-grandfather nodded silently—his joy making his ugly face glow. But that joy almost turned to despair when he tried to open her cage door and found it locked. He rattled the door three, four times but couldn't make it budge.

He loosed a low, sad groan but Mariana just gestured for my great-grandfather to step back. She then swung the door open without effort.

"It's only locked from the outside," she explained, as the two ran as fast as they could. "It's meant to keep you out, not us in."

They ran all the way back to my great-grandfather's house with Mariana carrying her broken shoes. They never told his parents—or their own daughter, for that matter—the whole story. Just that Mariana was a battered woman on the lam.

No one from the carnival ever came looking for Mariana.

"Why should they?" she said. "The world will never lack for people to gawk at."

The people from the small town took to her soon enough. (They already liked my great-grandfather, which made things easier.) And my great-grandparents married on what Mariana said was her 17th birthday.

My great-grandfather soon shed his title of "ugliest kid in the county" after Mariana appeared, though he never got any better looking. Instead, his friends and neighbors just called him The Smiling Man.

And, outside of the context of the fair and the show, no one ever called my great-grandmother a freak. The people of the town just thought of her as a sweet woman (who, admittedly, had a bit of a temper.) Maybe she was a bit homely but they figured she was still too pretty for her husband.

JASON LEA is a local editor for Mentor Patch, a news web site that covers suburban Northeast Ohio. It is often his job to talk to people on the worst day of their life. When he has the time, he prefers to write other things, as well. He has a wife named Jenny who is too good to him.

"I think a lot of beauty (at least, in the physical sense) is circumstantial. A lot of witches would be called princesses if we put them in a ballgown and gave them glass slippers. Similarly, some queens might be treated like witches if they were forced into an unflattering house dress and told to stir a cauldron.

Perhaps, as a male, my opinion is skewed; but I think most Loathly Lady stories aren't about a woman's physical transformation. They are about the man finally getting his perspective correct. The woman was beautiful all along. The man just didn't recognize it."

Tree Bark Magic

Alexandra Seidel

With skin strong and dark as tree bark guard my heart:
I was never like the other girls, there were no pearls
in my future. Paint-red lips and wind blown skirts
were the fancies of others.

I had burnt bark and ash to mark my dark face darker,
I worked the soot in to sting
the heart, to freeze the words still on their tongues
while they stared into my bubble cauldron
as I boiled in it
the sweat of the land, a potion, a blend

of so many herbs and ancient, witch-woven art.
I was the center-self of me, grown within like a tree,
I was the mage entombed in bark, my heart a root
sick for water. Watch:

I met her on a path of elderberry, or she me, out with the moon
when the dandelions flew in flocks. Her hair was
meadowsweet willow green watercress tiger lily, soft as cherry blossoms;
dark as cherry blood were her lips, long as reeds her legs.
To my dark witchling oak, she was a princess sapling blooming sharp and radiant.

Win me, wants my heart to cry through ages worth of rings.
Such things do not come without a price.
I stain your silk black with my ash, say I, green with my moss;
You loved my in the night, can you still look at me in the day?

The dandelions have shaken off their seeds, a charm
of hope and wind. We will see, she says, if you can love my milk-and-velvet hair,
can love me who never stirred a cauldron proper.
And she dips her fingers in the ash, paints black like a slash
of longing all along her cherry dream lips.

ALEXANDRA SEIDEL probably caught the myth and fairy tale bug while she was out in the woods one midsummer day. Meanwhile, the disease has turned her into a poet, writer, and editor. Her work may be found in *Strange Horizons, Jabberwocky, Stone Telling,* and elsewhere. You can follow her on Twitter (@Alexa_Seidel) or read her blog: www.tigerinthematchstickbox. blogspot.com.

"Why write about the Loathly Lady? Actually, why not. Why not explore the unexpected, the non-normative, the things many stories forget to mention, why not take this age-old, ephemeral thing—beauty—and ask what it really is, what it means to be beautiful?"

Seed Pearls
Jennifer Adam

Jason Gardner watched his bride turn to an ex in a cloud of satin and seed pearls as she ran through the church doors. Her parting words buzzed like wasps in his ears, stinging the back of his neck with an angry flush.

"I'm sorry, but I just can't do this," she'd said, not sounding sorry at all as she interrupted the minister. She turned to Jason, tugging the diamond ring he'd given her off a shaking finger and handing it back. "I can't. I can't let you dictate my life. I can't marry you."

The shocked silence that filled the church had muffled his tongue, forcing him to swallow twice and clear his throat before he could say, "But, sweetie, I've only tried to make you happy. This is what you wanted."

"No. No, it isn't. I wanted a private ceremony in the woods. You wanted a big formal wedding in a church. None of this—"she'd waved her bouquet, scattering rose petals—"is what I wanted."

"You're just nervous. I should have realized this would all be too much for you, but every bride feels shy on her big day. Let's just…"

"No. You're not *listening*. You never listen. You're so sure you know what I want; I never even get the chance to choose. Well, right now I'm choosing freedom. I'm sorry. I am." And Sarah had lifted her skirts to run like a star in a tawdry daytime drama, leaving him clutching a diamond that bit his palm with its broken-glass promise.

He went back to the apartment they'd shared and waited, sure she would change her mind. She just had cold feet, and once she had a chance to think things over she would realize how happy he made her. Hadn't he given her the life every woman wanted? Flowers and jewelry and pretty clothes, an apartment filled with classy furniture, and candlelit dinners at quiet restaurants.

She would come back.

She *had* to come back. All her things were still here.

Summer dried and crumbled at the edges, blew away in storm-gray gusts and drifts of dying leaves.

He started drinking.

He waited.

WINTER'S GLAZE FROSTED THE WINDOWS AND POWDERED SUGAR SNOW dusted the sidewalks, and still he waited.

Sometimes he smoothed his hands over the dresses hanging in her closet, the shirts and skirts he'd chosen for her.

She would be back.

He kept drinking.

ONE AFTERNOON, HE STAGGERED BACK TO THE APARTMENT AND KNEW she'd finally returned. Her perfume—some sweet simple scent she always wore no matter how many bottles of sophisticated fragrances he bought her—lingered in the air like the whisper of a kiss.

"Sweetie?" he tossed his keys in the basket by the door and strode into the open living space, a lofty room filled with the gloom of late December. "Where are you?"

She didn't answer.

Suspicion spider-legged down his spine and drew him to the bedroom.

The closet door was open and all her clothes were gone. He checked her dresser drawers and then he saw, in a velvet box upon the nightstand, the pearls he'd given her every year for Christmas. A set of earrings. A bracelet. Two strands, one of gleaming white, one of palest pink. A seed-pearl pendant on a thin silver chain.

Her tiny, elegant handwriting covered a piece of paper like lace at the bottom of the box and he gently teased it out from beneath the pearls. *"Jason,"* it read. *"I'm sorry I left the way I did, but the truth is, I don't even like pearls. What's that saying, about gilded cages? Anyway, I'm sorry and I wish you the best."*

That was it.

He stumbled to the kitchen and poured himself a drink.

THE DAYS BLURRED TOGETHER AT THE BOTTOM OF EVERY DIRTY GLASS and empty bottle, until two of the senior partners showed up at his door.

"Jason, look. We know you've been through a rough time, but you haven't worked a case in four months. You're falling apart. You need a change of scenery," Tom Harkin said, "a chance to regroup and get a hold of yourself."

"Take a few months. Find a quiet place in the country, get a hobby. Meet new people. Do whatever it takes, and then come back to the firm ready to win again. Okay?" John Larson, who'd hired Jason out of law school a decade earlier, said.

HE HADN'T MEANT TO BUY THE HOUSE CROUCHING LIKE A WARY CAT behind a yew hedge and old-fashioned wrought-iron gate, but somehow he hadn't been able to resist it. It was priced to sell, for one thing, and in the dusty corners of his mind he heard his father's voice telling him a little spit-polish and elbow-grease could turn a tidy profit if he decided to flip it later. But, really, there was just something about it, something that could have been called charm if you liked sagging porches and creaky doors and dust and cobwebs.

It looked like a story, or the memory of a story.

A haunted house ghost story, he amended, when a crow launched itself from the porch railing and startled him.

Sarah would love this place, he thought. *Wouldn't she?* But then, suddenly, he wasn't sure.

He discovered the garden after he'd already signed the papers and moved a few battered cardboard boxes in. He'd noticed the yard—dimly, from the corners of his eyes—and had been pleased by its size and gentle slope, but when he later took a walk around the edges of the property, he was inexplicably intrigued by the tangled, weedy mess he found on the south side of the house. Crooked stone walls bordered raised beds and, if he kicked away tendrils of ivy and tenacious thorny things he couldn't even name, he could see the remnants of a gravel walkway.

This garden had once been something special. He was sure of it, though he couldn't have said why he knew. He breathed the scents of crushed leaves, bruised petals and spring-warmed earth and decided to restore the garden to its former glory.

It was midmorning before Jason made his way back to the garden the next day. Bees buzzed their sunshine songs in the flowers growing wild around the base of a cracked birdbath and a cheeky robin tugged a worm from the soil not a handspan away from his shoe as he stood and surveyed the wonderland he'd found.

How did one go about taming a wild garden? He didn't even know where to start.

Rocking back on his heels, he studied the gnarled tree standing guard in the corner. It should be cut down first, that much was clear. It clawed the sky with twisted limbs and blackened twigs, like a sentinel of death. No spring sweetness quickened along its branches to mist them green with hope; it was barren and broken, casting a grim shadow over the garden.

The tree made him uneasy, if he cared to admit as much.

And if he cut it down, that side of the garden would be clear for a series of neatly spaced geometric beds, the sort that could make a proper garden from a tangled wilderness. Yes, that was the beginning.

He turned away from the apple tree—was it an apple tree? He really didn't know, but that's what he thought of when he looked at it—and hurried toward the garden shed he'd spotted behind the house. If he was lucky he might find the tools he needed.

The shed door was covered in a curtain of vines and the hinges were rusted, but he managed to clear a way in. The bare bulb hanging from the ceiling still worked and, despite the cobwebs and paper wasp nests clinging to the corners, the shed was surprisingly tidy. Shelves near the back wall held rows of clay pots, stacks of planting manuals and garden books, and small tools. A table stood in the middle of the space, and in a cabinet against the opposite wall he finally found a power saw.

He didn't know if it would start, but he was shockingly eager to try.

He hadn't taken two steps toward the apple tree when a bone-deep groan he felt as much as heard stopped him, rolling through his feet and down his spine.

The tree's branches writhed as if tossed by a storm, shrieking where old bark rubbed. Only, there was no wind.

Jason dropped the saw from fingers suddenly gone cold and lifeless, and the tree went still.

He blinked. Rubbed a hand across his eyes. Blinked again.

The tree looked as dead as it had a moment earlier, but now its branches stretched toward him, almost in supplication.

She doesn't want me to cut her down, he thought. And then wondered where the thought came from.

JASON LAY IN BED, GRASPING WISPS OF SLEEP THAT ONLY MELTED AWAY the minute they brushed his mind. He couldn't stop thinking about the apple tree in the garden.

It was strange, that tree. There was something... something *fey* about it. Echoes of old stories and fairy tales rustled in the corners of his memory and stirred restlessly beneath his skin.

It's just a tree and you have an overactive imagination, he told himself.

But every time he closed his eyes he saw those writhing branches again, felt the subliminal shriek as he'd approached with the chainsaw.

Finally giving up on sleep, he reached for a book on the nightstand only to realize he'd not yet unpacked anything to read. Clicking his tongue in irritation, he tossed the sheets off his legs and stood up. Instead of heading for the den to rummage through a box of dusty books, though, he pulled his pants on and hurried outside.

There were gardening books in the shed, he recalled. And since it was the garden—the tree in the garden, at any rate—that kept him from sleep, he might as well start learning what he could.

The ground was cold and dew-damp beneath his bare feet and goosebumps pebbled his skin. Rubbing warmth into his arms, he broke into a jog…

…and stumbled when he spotted the figure of a woman leaning against the gnarled tree in the garden. "Hello?"

She took a step farther out of the shadows, tilting her face to the moon as if she could feel its light on her lips and pale cheeks. Her hair hung over her shoulders in a mass of knots and frayed curls and—he couldn't help noticing—her legs were bare beneath a too-short skirt with a tattered hem.

"Are you okay? Can I help you?" he asked, uncomfortably aware of his own state of rumpled half-dress.

She lowered her gaze and her lips twisted bitterly.

"Wait! What's the matter? What's wrong?"

But she turned away, stepping back into the darkness at the base of the ugly old tree.

Worried now, Jason raced to the tree. Should he call the police? A neighbor?

But when he reached the tree, pressing a hand against the rough bark to steady himself, she was nowhere to be seen. He stared around stupidly, wondering where she could have gone. "Hello?" he called. A dog barked somewhere in the distance and he thought he heard an owl, but there was no sign of the strange girl.

Had he imagined her, the way he'd imagined the tree's reaction to his chainsaw? What was wrong with him?

"Maybe I'm having a nervous breakdown," he whispered. Beneath his palm, he felt the sudden flutter of a pulse—almost as if the tree had a heartbeat, as if the bark was skin.

Snatching his hand away, Jason ran back to the house.

IN THE GLARE OF DAYLIGHT IT WAS EASY ENOUGH TO CONVINCE himself he'd been half-asleep and seeing things, but he poured the last of his liquor down the kitchen drain anyway.

Tom Harkin called to see how he was getting on. "Got a case here you might be interested in. I'll fax you the details if you're up for it…"

Jason told him he'd be glad to take a look, and then talked about the garden and the girl he thought he'd seen the night before. After an awkward pause, Tom said, "Maybe the place is haunted. Maybe you've got your very own ghost."

But Jason heard what he didn't say, and was quick to assure him that he had quit drinking. "Besides, I don't believe in ghosts."

And he didn't.

WHEN HE WALKED PAST THE TREE ON HIS WAY TO THE SHED THAT afternoon, he noticed a place in the bark that looked exactly like the face of a young woman.

That explains it, then, he thought. A trick of the moonlight made it look even more real.

But after he'd tidied the shed and collected the gardening books and raked some of the fallen leaves away from the edges of the path, the face was no longer visible. Jason studied the tree from every angle, and could not see it.

⤜

HIS DAYS BEGAN TO FIT THEMSELVES TO A RHYTHM. HE DRANK HIS coffee on the back deck and spent the morning working in the garden. He cleared away the weeds, trimmed overgrown hedges, repaired the birdbath and replaced the old gravel paths with stepping stones. He planted flowers and ferns and bushes, filled with satisfaction at the feel of soil between his fingers.

He'd thought, a time or two, of trimming the apple tree's gnarled branches even if he couldn't bring himself to cut her down. But after a few weeks he had to admit she no longer looked like she needed pruning; the worst of her limbs seemed to have straightened themselves out and the tree was gaining a hint of grace. Though she hadn't bloomed, a few brave leaves unfurled along the ends of her branches to prove she wasn't dead yet.

Maybe knowing the garden was being put to rights gave the tree hope.

In the afternoons, he worked on trial documents and teleconferenced with his partners. Brick by paper brick he built a new life, integrating his old career with his new hobby until he could barely remember the time he'd spent in fashionably tiny apartments in the city.

In the evenings, when crickets and frogs sang the sun to sleep, he wandered back through the garden. It took him several weeks to understand the feeling rising in his chest every time a new flower bloomed or a new bud burst into green growth.

He was falling in love with his garden.

Sometimes he could see the face in the tree, and sometimes he imagined it was watching him.

⤜

THE LONGEST DAY OF THE YEAR LEFT A GOLDEN HAZE ALONG THE horizon that slowly coalesced until a ripe full moon rose, floating like a peach in a bowl of sky.

Jason sat in the garden, his back against the gnarled tree. Fireflies blinked in dusk-draped shadows and a light breeze stirred.

Twigs scraped behind him and he jumped.

Must be a rabbit, he thought.

But when he looked up, the girl he'd seen—or imagined—before was standing in front of him, nervously twisting her hands.

"I... I came to thank you," she said. Though her voice was rough—from lack of use?—an underlying sweetness made it pleasant.

Jason could have choked on his tongue, but he managed to stutter, "Thank me? For what?"

She smiled, waving a hand at the garden. "For this. For bringing my garden back to beauty."

"Your garden? But... who are you?"

Resting a hand lightly against her temple, she said, "I had a name once, but it's been so long since I had need of it... I do not remember what I was called." She frowned, and then shrugged off her dismay. With a gentle laugh, she said, "Now I choose my name. You may call me... Eve." And she laughed again, caressing a low-hanging branch of the tree.

"But... Eve... where are you from?"

She spread her hands and laughed again. "Here, of course. This is my tree, and my garden."

"I don't understand."

His brain was still stumbling over the impossibilities, picking at the knots. How had she simply appeared like that? And how could this be her garden when he'd bought it months ago? What on earth was she talking about; what did she mean?

Was she crazy? Or was he?

"You're having trouble with the lilies and the dahlias over there," she said, "because they don't like the bench stuck in their midst. There used to be a sundial there and they would much prefer another. You can move the bench here. I don't mind."

Bemused, he scratched his head and said, "Okay..."

"And if you would read to me, now and then, I would greatly

appreciate it. The wind has told me all its secrets and the birds are useless gossips. I've been hopelessly bored for ever so long..."

She shook her hair away from her face and raised her arms to the moon. "It still feels good to stretch, though I've lost interest in running as I used to..." Then, yawning, she leaned against the tree beside him and...

...disappeared.

Jason leaped to his feet, staring at the tree. One second she'd been standing there, plain as noon, and the next...

The face.

Had she been watching him from *inside* the tree?

❦

THE NEXT MORNING, FEELING SILLY AND STUPID, HE MOVED THE wrought iron bench to a spot beneath the apple tree. That evening, hoping none of his neighbors would see, he opened a book and began to read.

By the end of the week, he'd found a sundial at an antique store and placed it, carefully, among the fading lilies and dahlias.

In three days they had filled the bed with a profusion of glorious color.

❦

A WEEK LATER, EVE STEPPED FROM THE TREE AND SAT BESIDE HIM on the bench as he read to her. "You have a nice voice," she said, and leaned her head against his shoulder to listen.

He finished the book and asked if she would like another. "Tell me about your life," she said, and so he did. He told her about Sarah and her pearls and the day of his not-wedding.

"Pearls. I love pearls," Eve said wistfully. "She sounds like a wicked, selfish girl, to leave you like that." Her sidelong glance was sharp, glittering.

"No!" He startled himself by the force of his defense. "No, she wasn't at all selfish. She was desperate, I think. I... I thought that I loved her, and I was angry with her for not seeing it. But..."

"But what?"

"But now I think I loved who I wanted her to be. I wonder if I ever even really knew her."

Eve reached for his hand and squeezed his fingers.

And then she told him her story; how she'd wished for beauty so she could steal a man's love, and how she'd bought a spell without knowing the price of her vanity would be imprisonment within a tree.

"The spell wore off," she said, indicating her face, "but I'm still bound to this tree."

"I think you're beautiful," he said, and meant it.

SHE DID NOT APPEAR THE NEXT NIGHT, AND HE WAS AFRAID HE'D SAID something to offend her. Though it rained, he sat on the bench for hours, hoping she would leave her tree and keep him company.

He had not realized how lonely he was.

THERE WAS A JEWELRY STORE AN HOUR AWAY. HE BOUGHT SEVERAL strands of seed pearls and two pairs of earrings. Once home, he draped them over the branches of the apple tree and pressed the earrings into the soil at the base of the tree.

Then he sat on the bench and waited.

And waited.

She did not appear.

His heart broke and he thought about tearing away the pearls, but he could not make himself destroy something so beautiful.

"Please, tell me if I've done something wrong. What do you want from me? What do you need? Please. I miss you. I... I love you."

And he knew that it was true.

⚘

HE SPENT ALL NIGHT ON THE BENCH BENEATH EVE'S TREE. AND ALL DAY.

⚘

WHEN NIGHT CAME AGAIN, A PALE SLIVER OF MOON, NO BIGGER THAN a baby's fingernail, floated above the horizon and snagged in a wisp of cloud.

Eve stepped from the tree and flung her arms around him. "Oh, dearest, I would have come to you sooner, but moonlight is the only thing that can loosen my bindings and..."

"The storm," he said, understanding suddenly.

She nodded. "And last night was a dark moon. Even tonight..." she shuddered and clutched at him. "I am weak. The moon is too young. But I wanted to thank you for my pearls... they look like drops of moonlight." She touched a strand, setting the pearls shimmering. "And I wanted to tell you that I love you, too."

His heart leapt and he kissed her, tasting the apple sweet honey of her mouth and twisting his hands in her thick hair. She smelled of earth and apple blossoms, moonlight and roses and sugar.

He opened his eyes and caught his breath. She was glowing, her skin as luminous as if moonlight ran in her veins instead of blood. "Eve..." She was beautiful, in a way no other woman he'd ever seen could be.

She stepped away from him, her eyes wide and shining in the dark. She circled the tree, tracing patterns on the bark with her hand. "I am no longer bound," she said, her voice full of wonder. "I am free!"

"Does that mean you can stay with me? For good?"

Eve stood still, one hand still resting on her tree. "Oh, Jason. I love you. But..." she caressed the bark, touched a twig, brushed her fingers along a limb. "I have been part of this tree for a very, very long time. She will die without me, and I... I think a part of me would die without her, too. I cannot leave her..." Tears spilled down her cheeks.

He wrapped her in his arms. "You do not have to choose between me and the tree. If I can share your life, that is all I ask. Even if we only have our nights together..."

She leaned against his chest and whispered, "There is another way."

"What do you mean?"

"If you wanted to be with me... there is a way." And she lifted from around her neck a leaf suspended from a silk cord.

"I would do anything for you," he said. And knew he would.

"Even give up your freedom? Bind yourself to a tree the way I am bound?"

"Gladly." He kicked off his shoes, feeling the rich, warm earth beneath his toes. "You have chosen the shape of your destiny, and I would choose mine to match. But how is it possible?"

"The woman who put the spell on me gave me this." She held up the leaf. "Are you certain...?"

"Yes. With all my heart."

She kissed him and slipped the cord around his neck.

He felt himself stretching, reaching, growing, spreading until his limbs were entwined in the limbs of Eve's apple tree. He took a breath and... separated...himself from the tree, stepping out beside Eve.

They kissed in the moonlight while their trees waited for morning.

WHEN SPRING CAME, THE APPLE TREE BURST INTO FULL BLOOM WHILE the oak beside it stood guard.

JENNIFER ADAM lives with her husband and two children on a farm where coyotes sing and trees catch secrets in their branches. When she's not riding mustangs or dancing in the moonlight, she can be found with a book in her lap and a pen in her hand. Her work has previously appeared in *The Edge of Propinquity* and in a variety of equine journals.

"I often think about beauty, choice, freedom, and expectation and I enjoy playing with those themes in my writing. I'd had a nebulous story idea involving a woman, a tree, and pearls floating in my head for a while when I saw the announcement regarding the first issue of *Scheherezade's Bequest* and the theme of the Loathly Lady. I **love** different versions of that story, and I suddenly found all the vague elements of my own story starting to coalesce and take shape. I knew I wanted to write something that would examine conceptions of beauty, role expectations, and a woman's choice. This magazine gave me the perfect opportunity and inspiration, and I am deeply honored to be included in it."

TRUTH POWDER
Monika John

THE OLD WITCH LIVED HIGH ON A MOUNTAIN—FAR AWAY FROM THE people who shunned her unless they needed her healing herbs. Her back and shoulders were hunched, her eyes perpetually cast towards the ground as she was searching rock crevices for new healing plants. Her aim was to lighten the burden of human suffering and pain.

Even though her life was spent in serving others, those who received her help did not want to look into her face for all its ugliness. Her wiry hair was dull and gray, long strands hung down to her waist and covered most of her face. Her skin was parched and wrinkled from the harsh climate and her cheeks were sunken and hollow. Bitterness distorted her features.

Only one human being did not shun her as the others did—a small boy often came to hear stories of her long life. He had visited for many years now, yet his age and size appeared to remain the same over time. She had already told him many tales, and lone travelers sometimes heard haunting songs from a brittle old voice as they passed her hut. When they peered through the broken windows they would see an ancient hag sorting and drying her herbs with a little boy looking on.

One day the child visited again and watched her silently for a while as she ground dried purple leaves into a fine powder. This special herb—called the truth powder—was given when all other remedies failed. It grew only in one secret place on the steepest face of the mountain. A treacherous path led to the small patch. In winter the snow covered the ground around the herb but no frost ever touched it. People who tried to find it without guidance perished in the quest and fell to their death.

The old woman ground the powder so finely that a few specks escaped her earthen bowl and were inhaled by the little boy. Normally very young children were not affected by it, but this one, even though he did not appear old enough to have collected many untruths yet, had been taught to be polite and not to ask questions that embarrassed grown-ups, and that meant that he had already learned to keep things hidden inside. He sneezed when the powder tickled his nose, but it was too late and the one question he had honestly wanted to ask the old woman for a long time escaped his lips before he remembered what he had been taught. He looked straight into her eyes and asked:

"Why are you so ugly?"

Her eyes grew dark with anger as she gasped at his bold question. She would have banished him from the mountain forever, had she not—by gasping for air—inhaled a few grains of the powder herself. She coughed quickly to expel it from her throat but it was too late. It had entered her body and now she was bound to answer him truthfully. She sat down in her rocking chair and asked the boy to sit on the footrest in front of her.

"Long time ago," she began, "I lived on an island in the South Seas. I was very beautiful. Oh yes, I was! My hair was raven black and so shiny that the rays of the sun used it for a mirror. My skin was the color of olives, smooth like velvet. I sang all the time and my melodies rivaled the most wonderful bird songs. I painted beautiful fabrics with the bright yellow of the morning lily, the red of wild poppies and the blue of the cloudless sky. No one had seen such art before."

She sighed remembering.

"Yes, I was beautiful and proud and many men came to court me. I sent them away, especially the strong and handsome ones—my vanity could not bear to share admiration with anyone. Finally I chose one who was so humble that he walked behind me like a shadow. Oftentimes he was not even noticed in the room with me. He followed my every whim without complaint or reproach. I loved him as one might a faithful dog and soon began to find fault with his most insignificant gestures. How furious he made me with his obedient eyes!"

She winced at the memory of the man she had called husband.

"For many years I belittled him and with his weakness my power grew—at least it seemed so to me. I did not pay heed to the law which applies everywhere that holds: 'Even the tiniest ant crushed with malice, brings the wrath of the gods onto him who crushed it.' Another version is this: 'He who breaks carelessly and without respect the weak stem of a flower, will himself be bent in time to face the earth in darkness.' I never saw the punishment carried out immediately and therefore I did not believe in it. Its workings were invisible for many years and even decades.

My husband attended to me always like a faithful slave. He even admired me after my youth began to fade. He had watched my art for a many years and one day he took up the brush himself. The creatures he painted were oddly arranged in intricate and confusing patterns. He sat for hours and hours like a child drawing ugly characters. He hardly ate or slept and of course, did not devote his time to me. I grew more jealous with every day. My words to him became more spiteful, but he hardly heard me. He never talked back, just nodded as though he agreed with me and continued to draw. After three years of this I became ill and took to bed. I was weak and had trouble breathing. You see," she said touching the boy's shoulder, "I did not let him know that I was jealous of these ugly creatures, I always told him that I did not care if he stayed or left."

As the witch was telling her story, she noticed something strange about her small visitor. He seemed to have grown a few inches, but she just rubbed her eyes thinking she was imagining things and went on.

"I had noticed something peculiar about my own paintings just before my sickness. Here and there a few of my husband's deformed creatures crept in—they came out of the brush and appeared in the painting hiding under leaves or peeping out from under the flowing hair of an island maiden. Many travelers in the past had given me much silver for my paintings, but now they would look at them for a while and then turned away without buying anything. In the meantime, the colors in my husband's paintings became as brilliant as mine and one had to look closely to see the deformed creatures in the rich texture of his fabrics. I never understood those hideous things," she said, shaking her head still confused after all the years.

"He was angry," the boy said, "very, very angry! They were anger devils, don't you see?"

His voice was firm and the tone let her know that he was certain of his own words. Oddly enough he sounded like a young man. The old woman shook her head; her eyes were fixed on her gnarled hands. She assumed that her ears were failing her, as her eyes had before and she continued her tale.

"I became weaker as time went on. Finally my husband had to cease painting and again attend to me as he had done years before. He was afraid to lose me. He prepared my food with the greatest care and watched over me day and night. He was often tired but the moment he would rest I told him that I was thirsty or hungry and he got up and did my bidding. Together we went to many healers. No one could help me. One of them told me that only my heart was sick and nothing else; then she turned and walked away. I felt death approaching.

We became more afraid and decided to seek out a woman who had visited our island a few years before. I did not know at the time that she was a Truth Dreamer. She brought healers to me, those who cure body and soul, but again nothing helped, perhaps because I sent every one away after a day or two, not believing in them longer than a few hours.

The woman had become very quiet and was watching me with great attention. And she had dreamt about me—I felt it. Then one day she stood before me and said,

'You are not healing because you do not wish for it. Your illness serves your purpose and you have brought it unto yourself by the harmful words you have spoken in your life and still continue to speak. Until you accept the truth of this, there is no hope for you.'

I was furious and cursed her for being cruel to a dying woman. As always my husband agreed with me and both of us left her home immediately. The last words she spoke to me were these,

'May you find forgiveness for all the taking you have done in your life.'
Then she turned to my husband and said,
'May you find forgiveness for all the giving you have done.'
She bowed and closed the door behind us.

Suddenly the witch's tears were flowing with remorse. She finally understood the words spoken by the Truth Dreamer. She brushed aside a strand of hair that had fallen in her face. It was jet black. Her eyes became round with surprise when she looked at the young man sitting in front of her. His features were so familiar and yet...

He touched her hand which was no longer so bony and emaciated.

"Do you remember anything else?" he asked.

"Afterwards, we moved from place to place, seeking out new cures, holy places and healers, everywhere I was told that I could not be helped. And all the time, my husband served me," sobbed the witch. "He served me without complaint even though he was dreadfully tired. Oh, how mean I was to him!" she could hardly speak for all the tears that were now like a river flowing and swelling with honest shame.

"He served you for his own purposes and not because he cared for you," the man in front of her said with conviction, all childishness gone from his voice. "He had never wanted to grow up. By nature he was lazy. By following you and carrying out your demands, he never had to think for himself nor be responsible for his life. He could stay a child forever. What else do you remember?"

"Not much," she answered, "after some time we were so tired we lay down under a tree and fell asleep. I had a most wondrous dream. I saw a high peaked mountain and on one side, protected from the harsh cold winds, a patch of star-shaped purple flowers was growing. The mountain spoke to me: 'Not until you take these flowers into your own self will you find health and forgiveness.'

I decided in my dream to tell my husband to seek the powder for me but I never awoke under the tree again. Instead I found myself on this harsh mountain and so ugly that even the crows shriek in horror at the sight of me. I did find the purple truth powder and used it to heal others for so many years, that I can't remember. I never took it myself—until now I had forgotten the mountain's voice in my dream."

The man in front of her sat with his head bowed to the floor. After a while he said,

"I, too, had a dream in which the mountain spoke to me, but I don't recall what it said. I also woke up away from the tree. I found myself in the valley below. My body had become small. I was a child. A family took me in and gave me food and shelter. But I could not grow up—no matter what they did for me. I cursed my helplessness, cursed my endless days of play, my having to follow what the grown-ups told me to do. Oh, how I wanted to choose for myself and be responsible for my own life!"

Deep anguish lowered his voice and loosened a torrent of tears that flooded his heart and carried away the helplessness of uncounted years.

The misery and remorse of the two called in the Laughing Sorrowbird, a most peculiar little feather ball, who watched them cry for a while and then exploded into the most contagious laughter. His laughter echoed through the mountains and rang with a thousand voices until the two could not resist any longer and began to laugh through their tears. All sadness was swept out of their hearts.

"Well," the woman said, wiping her eyes dry and added still laughing, "That is the tale of my ugliness."

"Ugliness?" the man protested. He was fully grown. "Look!" He held a mirror up to her face.

The glass reflected a radiant face with smooth olive skin and fine features. And a thousand and one sunrays shone through a crack in the wooden roof and bounced and danced through her raven black hair.

Dear wounded Friends,

Wish you did, wish you might have
learned the truth between you,
then this story could be true already.
Honest regret would have given
strength of heart and beauty for ashes.

But even your failure is only a sleeping.
Truth has already spoken
grace over your brokenness
and your awakening will come
at the appointed hour.

–Truthdreamer

MONIKA JOHN's own search for truth and her interest in different cultures and world religions took her to different continents from Africa, South America, China, Southeast Asia to India. She encountered the main characters of the 'Truth Powder' in Polynesia. Her writings appeared in various journals in the US and UK. Her most recent poems were published by Sampad in partnership with the British Council in the anthology *Tagore Inspired, Buddhist Poetry Review, Quiet Shorts Magazine, Presence International Journal of Spiritual Direction, Fungi, Urthona Magazine UK, Penwood Review, Sathya Newsletters*, and she has work forthcoming in *Crone* and *Lalitamba Magazine* (NY). Monika was born in Europe. She is an attorney who practiced law in California until she moved to an island in the Pacific Northwest.

"This is a tale about a 'Loathly Lady" but one who did not require a kiss from a friendly prince to morph from ugly caterpillar into a beautiful butterfly. All she needed was a little truth powder. The story wrote itself when an artist friend died around age 40; she could not bear to lose her beauty; her husband was a man who would not grow up. Had they found a bit of truth between them perhaps she could have lived and he might have found maturity. In gaining insight in the 'Truthpowder' he grew up and she recovered her inner and outer beauty. Truth is Beauty."

Old & Cursed

Rebecca-Anne C. Do Rozario

Hank Mutt left his apartment, dragging his fifty one years behind him like so much faded bunting from a birthday party. He pulled up the hood of his plastic rain cloak, pulled on his dark green wellies and headed down Hurricane Lane, swinging from crooked lamp post to crooked lamp post like a mythical great ape, rain whipping up from the paving stones to slop over his boot tops and soak his socks.

He turned into Snowfalls Parade and shivered. It was always just so cold in Snowfalls Parade. He hunkered down a little further into his layers of blue and grey, thinking about the woman who lived above the ice vendor at number twenty-one. They'd dated once. She was beautiful and clever and she liked leprechaun polka non-ironically too, but she broke it off, saying something about a prior commitment to a goblin. A snowball plummeted into the back of his head, but he didn't flinch. It was the kind of thing you expected. The explosion of white powder revealed a golden framed miniature that had been at the centre of the frozen missile. It was swiftly buried in a drift by the door of Wool & Ribbons, the pale face within the frame elegantly smothered, unnoticed.

Once he stepped into Sunshine Road, he shook the wet off the plastic cloak and wadded it up roughly into a bundle to carry under his arm. The drying plastic creaked and crinkled as he strode along under the sunny sky, spied between the rows of cheerful iron lacework on the upper floors of the shops and houses. He quickly loosened his woven scarf from around his chin, ruffling out his grey curls. A smile fleetly twitched his lips. When he looked into his chatty mirror that morning, he could see his face in its inexorable meltdown, slipping slowly and softly into grizzled folds. "You're showing your age," it told him, a trifle smugly. "But Bob the Gnome down in Thunder Square is showing his age even more." Hank recklessly pulled his shirt open at the throat, the shiny buttons catching the light. The small triangle of his pale chest practically glowed in the warmth of the sun. He still had enviable proportions, lean, but with wide shoulders and large, very manly hands, thanks to his elfish genes. His mirror could slight him first thing in the morning, but he could still charm a Dowager or Fairy Godmother by supper time.

He flicked his scarf back up around his neck as he headed into Stormy Avenue, his feet splashing along the cobbles. He dodged a dark cloud, bubbling and roiling, tethered to the street hydrant. They weren't usually armed with lightning bolts, but occasionally one would spit one out across the street, frying anyone in the way. Hank stepped smartly by and stopped at a bright green kiosk. He dug into his pockets and produced a copper coin, flipping it to a woman in a tall, black hat. She in turn flipped a tap at the bottom of a steaming cauldron, handing him a paper cup of espresso. It scalded his tongue, but he didn't mind. He thanked her and stepped over to the noticeboard lurking behind the kiosk.

Small pieces of paper fluttered safe behind a glass screen. They carried details of dogs in need of rescue. There were mostly ordinary dogs, bright puppies, wise old dogs with whom he readily identified. Little blurbs gave their tales, wanting only happy ever afters. At the far corner of the board, however, were rarer categories like Cunning, Transformed and Familiar. Hank liked to look at the board. He always felt a towering eagerness to rescue all the dogs listed, though he knew that was impossible. He didn't have shining armour enough for such a task, let alone a supply of kibble and chew toys. Yet seeing their portraits and the promises of scratchable tummies and games of fetch, he felt the kingdom was made a more noble place. He laughed at himself and with one hand, jiggled loose his plastic cloak, tossing it over his shoulders as the rain stuck his curls to his jowls and the fleshy tips of his pointy ears. Continuing to sip his drink, Hank ran his finger down the edge of the board, one slip of yellowing paper beyond the glass rising to his touch.

He glanced at the category. "Old & Cursed Dogs."

The portrait was a mere sketch: a little old dog with buggy eyes, out of control, hoary brows, a balding muzzle and patchwork coat. Her long pink tongue hung out in already unremembered enthusiasm. Hank read her tale, "A loathly lady. We don't know her name. She lived with an ancient hag who died before she could pass it on. This little old lady is a bit incontinent and she has bad hips, but she is extremely loving and intelligent. She is looking for a place to live out her final days in peace and tranquillity..."

"And the occasional walk to pick up an espresso."

Hank turned around. A woman stood behind him, carrying a big wicker basket on one arm and an umbrella in the other hand. A chimera's head decorated the umbrella handle and the two bits of green glass in its eyes perfectly matched the colour of the woman's eyes, which stared right through him.

"Excuse me?" said Hank politely.

The woman tilted her head towards the board. Her dark hair was piled high in a top knot decorated with a pink gerbera and generous spray of gypsophila. She had a little snub nose and a rosy pout. Hank had the nagging feeling he should recognise her.

"I'm just looking," Hank said.

"Yes. You frequently just look." She offered him the basket. "It's time you acted. It's your destiny, if you insist." Hank looked confused. She sighed with an irritable snippiness, the point of her shiny shoe tapping on the sleek cobblestone beneath her foot. Hank felt peculiarly impelled to take the basket. It immediately barked at him. "She likes you."

Gingerly lifting the red cloth that covered the contents of the basket, Hank found himself staring into a big pair of melting, adoring, buggy eyes. It was the loathly lady, only the texture of her coat was more frizzled, her breath more pungent, her panting more wheezy than her tale had promised. He almost dropped the cloth, but before the edge left his fingers, she cocked her head, one flappy ear catching the wind. He smiled and scratched her ear for her, a reflex that overcame repulsion. A back leg vibrated with her delight and sold the deal.

"It's the same dog..." he began, but realised he was speaking only to the rain and that actual small, very ugly dog. "Well, I guess I am your knight in shining armour after all." She possibly meant it well, but in her enthusiasm, she released quite a bit of gas. Her ears drooped and Hank let go a remarkably high giggle for such a large man. "So, I was going to spend the day drinking with trolls up by Tornado Bridge, but I guess I'd better get some dog biscuits and maybe a few bones instead?" The dog gave a croaky bark and curled up in her basket again, proceeding to snore.

Hank was a pragmatic man and he reasoned that although he certainly hadn't decided to keep the dog, she, in turn, had certainly not had a say in being left with him. So he went about the city, filling a sack with the supplies the shop keepers insisted he'd require. He woke her up when they were back on Hurricane Lane in front of his building. The small dog grunted and stretched her short, arthritic legs, wagging her tail with curiosity. She really was *very* ugly.

Hank lived above the wind-maker's, where he worked from time to time, crafting squalls mostly. The shop awning bucked and billowed in the gale the apprentices were currently testing, a selection of chimes dancing and clanging along the edges of the canvas.

"It's going to be a noisy night," said Hank, who was shielding the basket with his plastic cloak. "Do you need to... you know... have a little privacy? There's some grass out back, but it's pretty waterlogged. You'll need wellies of your own and I think that's the only thing the seelie girl didn't try to sell me." His smile crinkled the lines around his eyes till his eye balls all but disappeared. He looked particularly charming. The dog barked happily. "Come on, my lady, you can talk to me..."

"Yes, I can," she said with a gentle cough to clear her throat. "But I'm cursed, remember? You had to release my words before I could speak."

The basket tipped dangerously on Hank's arm, a quite natural response to his amazement. He had not expected one of the magical dogs. For a start, magical dogs were pure bred, right little terriers. Most magical dogs lived in the palace and those who lived outside the palace were rare and much prized. Magical dogs decided who would care for them. Magical dogs did not end up on rescue lists.

The dog placed her plump paws on the edge of the basket, steadying herself. "I suggest we get in out of the rain and wind, Mr. Mutt?"

Hank took the stairs two at a time and fumbled his front door lock. Inside, he carefully placed her basket on his parlour rug while he doffed his cloak and boots and, after a moment of reflection, his soaked socks. As he did so, the dog wiggled half way out of her receptacle and gave a tired whine. Hank bent low and helped her properly out, her bad hips clicking.

"Thank you, Mr. Mutt," she said, tail wagging lopsidedly. "I'm Lady Mabel. I'm afraid you have a rather bad bargain of it. I'm really not the dog I once was..."

"I don't know about that," said Hank. "It's not every day you have the opportunity to rescue a venerable damsel. Hungry?"

"I could eat a bite."

Hank slipped into the kitchen, dropping his sack by the icebox and frowning at left over noodles from the Jasper Castle. It didn't seem like very good food for a noble dog, no matter how ugly she was.

"Who was that strange woman?" he asked, voice muffled by a selection of broccoli, ambrosia and several soft cheeses.

Lady Mabel was examining the spare furnishings. The sofa was stiff and covered in an unaesthetically pleasing brown material. There were two leather bound books on the half-log coffee table, *An Ogre's Guide to Weather Systems* and *Travels in Carabas*. Lady Mabel sniffed and began to inspect the low slung rocking chair, made from hundreds and thousands of walnut shells carefully hammered out and pressed together. It was made comfortable with a variety of rag-patched cushions and a rather horrible afghan knitted by a forgotten aunt. Wheezing and grunting, she climbed up onto the seat and curled there, generating a gentle rocking motion. Within moments, she was snoozing again.

Hank returned with a portion of cold beef on a plate.

"Lady Mabel?" he called softly.

She raised her head and sniffed at the beef. "Not bad, Mr. Mutt. I think I'd like to claim this chair, if that's okay with you? The locomotion is most convivial." She scratched an ear with her back leg. "I hope that's not a flea. Were you asking about my fairy godmother?"

Hank crouched down beside her, a worried frown working its way into his forehead. "You're not really a girl in there, are you?" He could see all sorts of complications arising if she were.

She hiccupped a chuckle. "Not at my age. And I'm the wrong size. Dogs have fairy godmothers too, you should know. Some of us truly need them. My life, after all, hasn't all been beer and pickles, Mr. Mutt. Do you have radio?"

"No. Reception in the city is bad. All the conflicting weather. They get a bit of a signal over in Sunshine Road and some parts of the Drizzle District, but..."

"Pity," said Lady Mabel with a large yawn that threatened to turn her inside out. "I used to like to fall asleep to Mr. Sandman's Lullabies. But that life is over." She sighed, her ears hanging low. "My poor hag. Good night, Mr. Mutt. I don't think..." She buried her head between her paws and her breathing slowed to a drawn out rasp.

And so Hank found himself quietly moving about his own home, avoiding banging pans or rattling dishes, slamming doors or splashing in his bath, all to accommodate the small, excruciatingly ugly dog who had been delivered to him in a basket.

He was woken that night at 2:47 a.m. His bedside clock, lit by will-o'-the-wisp and so one of his more expensive possessions, told him so exactly. Over the roar of another test-gale, he could here the unmistakable howl of a small dog. He was still wiping sleep from his eyes, so did not attend to its peculiar countermelody nor the sweetness of the higher register.

"Arrrrrrrrrrrgh..."

Stumbling over leather poufs and piles of laundry, Hank made his way into the parlour where he saw a dog sitting up by the skylight, her nose pointed to the heavens.

He rubbed his curls, looking everywhere for Lady Mabel and finally burst out, rather irrationally and sleepily, to the interloper, "What did you do with my dog?"

The little terrier looked down at him from atop the bureau. She was about the size of Lady Mabel and obviously also quite aged, but her platinum coat was soft, full and shimmered in the faint glow from the overhead skylight, her nose was wet and black, her eyes were a clear brown beneath tidy fringes. She was one of the most beautiful dogs he'd ever seen.

"Mr. Mutt, did I wake you?" she asked.

Hank tried to shake the remnants of a dream about half naked sirens and a record player from his head. "You were howling."

"Yes, I'm trying to catch the attention of the moon. I'd like to see the moon. And maybe some stars. But there's all that cloud and rain in the way." She popped down the staggered drawers of the bureau, carefully and slowly, with great grace and tenuous dexterity.

Hank stared at her for a few moments and then yawned, stretching the corners of his mouth and giving himself several additional chins. After yawning, he felt a little more awake. "You're Lady Mabel, aren't you? *This* is your curse."

She sat on the rug, gingerly arranging her hips, the tips of her perfect triangle ears flickering. "Does that discombobulate you?"

He scratched his head. "A little. It's a common enough curse. Yet, I've never seen someone so..."

"Old?"

"...old, yes. Someone so old and still cursed. Usually the curse is broken before... you know... you get old."

"Yes, the easiest way to break the curse is to berate some poor soul into bonding with you when you're positively repulsive." Lady Mabel sounded testy. "I didn't like to use the threat of life with me as a curse-breaker." She gave her ruff a good scratch, revealing her perfect white teeth and pink tongue. "And... to be honest, I've simply never met anyone I'd want to bond with. It happens. I went to live with the hag. My family were always trying to concoct love affairs for me. The hag suggested that I didn't have to choose between being grotesque and adorable. I've observed that it's different for fairies and gnomes and people and elves and all, but for dogs, ugliness is not such a crime. Most dogs go by smell and the most interesting smells are usually quite appalling. Five day old fish left out in the sun, the dung of an ogre, the pies that Mrs Paddyrod makes..."

"I think I get the picture," said Hank. "Or at least the scent."

"Does it bother you? Would you prefer me like this by day, when you're walking me?"

"Well, I expect I don't mind. Your bug eyes and motley coat have character. And... I'm not getting any younger. According to my optometrist, I'll probably be seeing you through four inches of glassware soon. Are you happy to be seen with a man whose face takes a whole morning to fall into place and who groans when he gets up off a chair?" Mabel's tale had begun to wag. It snapped back and forth rapidly and her tongue lolled out happily. She launched herself at Hank and licked him from brow to jowl and then again for good measure. "Hey, calm down."

"We're going to have such a great life together, Hank. And if we ever get caught in an experimental tornado, I'm your dog."

Hank laughed, throwing his head back. As he did so, he spied a woman with bright green eyes riding through the gale in a pumpkin dirigible. He had hoped to avoid entanglement with the fairy godmothers in his lifetime, but it was a small price to pay for having Lady Mabel in his life at last.

REBECCA-ANNE C. DO ROZARIO is teacher at Monash University, lecturing in English Literature. She has published a range of scholarly work on fairy tale, fantasy, children's literature and musical theatre in journals like *Women's Studies in Communication, Marvels & Tales,* and *Children's Literature.* Her work has also appeared in books including *The Gothic in Children's Literature: Haunting the Border.* She is usually accompanied by a very sociable Scottish Terrier and a bag full of knitting.

"I often browse pet rescue sights and the old dogs, their faces full of such fun and wisdom, always catch my eye. When the theme of the loathly lady came up, I thought about those dogs, old dogs with incontinence issues and arthritic joints, and also ugly dogs who don't know or care that they aren't attractive as long as you'll pat them or toss them a ball, all looking for new homes and people to love them and I wanted to write a tale about them. Not everyone or every dog has the choice to be more attractive, but I think we all deserve having people to love us in our lives."

THE DISPOSSESSED

Wendy Howe

Then she turned beautiful in her madness,
spell caster of strength and sorrow, dark moods
and strange dreams...
> *said of the village outcast*

Homeless, she haunts one place
than the next—
> dwelling in some neighbors' cellar
> or shed.

Her clothes are borrowed, her skin light
as the muslin sheet
> that wraps their dead.

She scrubs the rib bones
of a squirrel, an ivory comb

> for detangling
> her long hair,

and strews heather between
her bodice strings

> to guard herself
> against any curse or stare.

A candle defines her shadow
more often
than the slant of the sun.
> Alone,

she has mastered darkness
> learning why

the spider's veil is corner-spun.

WENDY HOWE is a writer who lives in Southern California with her partner. She is haunted by an interest in human nature, diverse landscapes and other invisible wonders of life. Over the years, she has been published in an assortment of journals both on-line and in print. Recently, her work has been showcased in four anthologies which feature a variety of women writers, *Lilith, Postcards From Eve, Tipping The Sacred Cow* and *Vintage*.

"The *loathly lady* theme appealed to me because of its diverse interpretation and my empathy for the outcast, recluse, psychic or nomad who becomes shunned and labeled because of her strangeness, a negative identity imposed upon her by others. Yet, beneath this stereotyped image, her vulnerability combined with a fierce tenacity to survive, evokes a heroic beauty. Something which enhances the human spirit and fortifies the will to live and choose freely. Something that may unsettle others (at first) but draws their fascination over time and even their envy.

Though fictitious, my character is loosely based on the woman who was treated as an outcast, seen as a threat to the moral welfare of the community and condemned as a witch in 17th century Salem, Massachusetts. Despite her willfulness, strange manner of dress and speech, Sarah Good still craved the right to be recognized with dignity, to be loved and valued. In her struggle and defiance, she becomes somewhat mythical and a significant influence on both literature and culture."

Skin Like Carapace

Steve Toase

I SLEEP SHALLOW AND MY MEMORIES WHISPER IN MY EAR, THEIR HAND on my shoulder so I cannot evade them. They speak to me of the first time I came to the market of fragrance, sixteen years old and face bare apart from one age branch carved above the broken brow of my nose. I pay them no heed, but it's hard, hard to ignore the first taste of the air surrounding the market. Then and still the greatest wonder of the Land of No Light.

Here you can buy powders to stain your skin with the scent of fly agaric and birch bark, or smoke to disguise you as a freshwater pool to hide from violent and determined creditors. Every day, between the fourth and the fifth bell, dancers gather on the cobbled square. Each one is bathed since birth in a different essence. They weave their scents into epic stories of the origins of the four Royal houses, and the spectres whose tattered odour is carried on the wind. Those who brush against the dancers never clean that patch of skin and carry the story on them throughout their lives.

If I concentrate I can still smell the tang of blood from my scuffed knees and feel the sting from picking pea grit from my scabs. Those times when my voice was too cracked to keep me on my feet. But those scars were trivial. With the help of older traders I soon learnt to navigate between the stalls by the click of my tongue and the brush of fungus that grew on the worn oak boards.

That was a long time ago and now I am not a young man. I sit in the centre of the market in a patch of crumbled marsh salt and tall wild garlic. No-one can enter without a Royal Warrant and no one can leave without being turned to silence. I can hardly smell the market now. The anise, cinnamon and sage no longer reach me, drowned out by the perfumes leaking from my body and staining my clothes.

Some time has passed since the Royal guards brought me here. How much I'm no longer sure. I've tried to keep track of the bells, of the ebb and flow of trading. Each session flows into the other and I lose track so easily. It was an accident. I think they know that so they guided me here with gentle hands rather than dragging me in chains.

The day was hot and my hands sweated up as I poured oils and tinctures. That was why the bottle slipped from my grip. The embossed glass smashed and spilt the Queen's scent over the poor girl walking by, soaking her rags with frankincense and saffron, sandalwood and ambergris.

Sellers and buyers alike approached her, smelling the perfume of their Regent, grasping her clothes and running their fingers across her forehead, surprise overriding any sense of etiquette. Instead of the arcing inscription scars of the Royal family they felt only shallow indentations of a house with no name. Their hands found no silk threaded embroidery, no pearls warming to their touch, or alencon lace finer than breath, only the tattered rags of a starving girl. Rumours spread of the Queen appearing in the market wearing tattered linen, and ash to grit her skin. Skin that was cold to the touch from the lack of fine robes. Seven satires were composed by street musicians and four caricatures carved into soapstone, each coated with a wash of frankincense and wood ash.

After I was taken no one knew or asked what happened to the girl, but not an hour goes past when I don't think of her and my collusion in her fate.

There is still time for me to run, to hide. To take handfuls of river mud and scrub my skin until my scent is worn away. I could conceal myself between footstep and speech, an outlaw. But who would I be then, a perfumer with no scent? To run would mean never smelling the haze of the market again, never becoming drunk on the mix of musk and oakmoss. Instead I will wait for the judgement of the Queen and hope she is merciful. I am not a young man and I am too tired to run.

I listen as the Queen's Justice approaches, trailed by her twelve servants. First they walk across the cloister, where trinkets of lavender are sold from rough-woven blankets. Their feet crunch on sand made of a million empty seashells. Next they cross the gravel path. I can hear mumbles of conversations and their boots scuff up small sprays of grit. They pass through the cobbled square, smooth soles slipping on the rounded stones. They are talking about me, though I know any decision will have already been reached. As one creature they cross the turf to stand around me. Their breath is controlled and shallow. I can taste it on the air, pungent with alcohol and calilaysa.

The Queen's Justice approaches the garlic patch, crushing the plants underfoot and leaning in close. Reaching up I run the pad of my palm across the woman's face. I feel where age and the inscriber's chisel have turned her beautiful, marking out her life. First I trace the lines of her office, the curving fronds of the royal seal, then the tree of age rising up the centre of her forehead, following the inscriptions marking journeys and lovers. Finally I bring my hand down to her mouth, touching the impressions marking each laugh and frown. The Justice returns the greeting, her long fingers reading the carvings across my face, pushing into my beard to touch the scars hidden on my cheeks. She grips my neck just under my chin.

"My mistress could have you turned to silence, your scent ground into the dirt underfoot and your marks wiped from all memory," the Justice says. "Instead she will give you a chance to redeem yourself. Succeed and you can return to your work, though you will never again serve the Royal Court. Fail and you will be turned to silence."

"And if I don't accept?" I say, although I know the answer. The Justice says nothing.

I tense my neck muscles in acknowledgement and the Justice lets her hand smile against my skin.

"Before the end of trading you must answer this question. What is everywhere yet has no scent?"

Then there is just the sound of breathing and I listen as the Justice and her twelve servants leave. There is still time to run, but I am not a young man and I have no heart for it.

Left alone I think over her words and think over the riddle. The question makes no sense. I am a master perfumer in the market of fragrance and we are taught young that everything has a scent and we learn young how to extract it. We can take tinctures from fossilised shells, from your lover's touch, from your child's amniotic soaked first breath and your lover's regret laden last. There is nothing in the Land of No Light absent of scent, and knowing this I start to prepare myself for silence. I am not a young man and maybe it is time to no longer be.

Yet I try to ignore the hopelessness of my situation and ask those who pass my confinement. I speak to traders who gather because they have know me since I first stumbled between their bouquets of dried flowers, and I ask those who gather out of morbid curiosity. No-one has an answer for me. They drift away through guilt, though the causes of their conscience are a world apart. I find myself alone again and try to come up with an answer, but every object and creature I bring to mind has its own taint and stench. With no hope left, I sit listening to and inhaling my home for one last time.

I hear her first, shuffling at the limit of my internment. She smells of condensation and death-watch beetles.

"You must leave," I say in a whisper. I don't want another life on my conscience, even as I teeter on the edge of losing my own.

"I can answer your riddle for you," she says. Her voice sounds like the throwing of bones, desiccated and rotten.

She moves closer and takes my wrist. Her skin is as smooth as carapace. She runs my hand across her face and I find nothing. No marks of office or inscriptions of achievement, no engravings of shared jokes and private sorrows, just blank, smooth, flesh stretched across bone, taut with emptiness. Bile rises from my stomach as my hand finds her face bare of marks. I can feel the acid burn my throat and taste it age my teeth. No-one is without a past or story. Even newborns carry the scars of birth, yet her face is absent of all of this. From the set of her jaw and razor cut of her cheekbones I know she is no child. I want to take handfuls of grit and scrub my palms down to the bone in case whatever disease afflicts her, whatever curse that has wiped her skin embryo clean, infects me. Better to let flames lick and blister my skin into strands of living liquid than touch her face. I try to bury my disgust and carry on, though she cannot be ignorant of my feelings. I am not a young man and have never been good at hiding my emotions.

I bring my hand over her mouth and feel no breath, only the wet, slow touch of her lips against my fingers. Trying not to flinch I take hold of her wrist and bring her hand in turn to my face, letting her read me. Her touch is slow and invasive. It takes all my will not to run as far as the entangled plants and crushed salt will let me.

"I can answer your riddle for you," she says again, her voice no warmer.

"And what do I give in return?"

"If you don't get the answer you will be reduced to silence. Surely any price I ask of you will be less than that?"

I think on this, and am not convinced she speaks the truth, but hers is the only help that has come and I have never claimed to be wise. I place her hand on my neck and tense my muscles in agreement. She clasps my hand, fingers between fingers, and moves our grip to the oath scar on my left cheek. She speaks first.

I pause, unsure if I have heard correctly, then repeat the words. "I swear that if the answer saves me from silence we will be married." I am a master perfumer and know any answer given will be wrong.

She leans in close and whispers the solution to me. I know as she speaks that this woman with no history, no inscriptions or crow's feet to bring beauty to her face, has given me the correct answer to save me from being reduced to silence. In that moment I know if I give her answer to the Queen's Justice then I will be released from my confinement and this woman will be my wife.

"I will leave now and return as your betrothed after you have given your answer to the Queen's Justice," she says, and I listen to her go.

Do not think that I am not considering giving the wrong answer. What value are honour and oaths when I will no longer exist to care? But something stops me and instead I sit waiting for the end of the market and the Queen's Justice to return.

They come as the sound of bartering lulls. I know the traders and sellers are waiting to hear my fate. I can taste them breathing though they still their lungs. The Queen's Justice and her servants have scorched corpse hair and animal pelts against hot stones and dressed themselves in the smoke. They mute their shoes, but to me they sound like a storm gathering.

The Justice steps onto the salt and wild garlic and we exchange greetings.

"Do you have an answer for me?" she says, and for a moment I think I detect a hint of regret in her voice as she places her hand against my neck. I tense my muscles.

"What is everywhere and has no scent? I caution you to answer carefully as only one answer can be given."

I pause. Some think I do this for effect, but I am not a young man and it takes time to gather my thoughts.

"Sound," I say.

A gasp goes through the crowd like an echo, starting with the Queen's Justice and spreading backwards to the far reaches of the market.

The next few moments feel like an anticlimax, even for me who can now go on living. The Justice takes my hand and leads me from my confinement and the inscriber is called forward to add a new mark to my face. It takes much searching to find the symbol. Many markets have met since anyone left the garlic alive. Certainly it has not happened in my time. The blood from my new scars reminds me of scuffed knees all those markets ago. I allow myself a moment of relief, but it is short lived.

"Where is my husband to be?" my saviour calls out from the cobbled square.

I think about ignoring her. The punishment for oath breaking is the loss of a hand. Surely that is less of a burden than a wife I do not want? A wife who is so without experience that she does not bear one mark. Then I hear her cry taken up by others.

"Where is this woman's husband to be?" and the gossips go to ask her story.

Before long the market is noxious with it. I have little choice but to approach her and acknowledge my oath.

The wedding is short and over quickly and I do not wish to dwell on it here.

She moves into my home and I feel like she's everywhere. I go to bury my clothes and boots, stained as they are with the herb of silence and brittle salt. When I leave her alone she recovers them and I resent her for it.

We bed down in separate rooms. I say my back hurts, or my hands are so soaked in tinctures that they will burn her skin if we embrace. While she sleeps I dab diluted perfume behind her ears. Too subtle for most to sense, even my new bride, but I can smell it and leave any room she enters. I do not want to convulse in her presence. I'm disgusted by her, but I am not a young man and try to hold onto some manners. This way I carry on as before, though another Perfumer dresses the Queen's skin. A small price compared to others I pay.

She asks to come to the market with me, to sell scents to the gentry, and crush spices for me.

"Imagine how many more beautiful perfumes you could make with two of us working on your stall," she says.

"Not today," I say. "I have a delivery of herbs coming and there is little enough space for me." "I am mixing today. If you knock over the tinctures our livelihood will be gone." "I have an important buyer coming and need to give him my full attention."

She does not believe these excuses and neither do I. How can I tell her that if she came to the market and someone exchanged greetings with her I would be a laughing stock. I have little enough trade as it is. Few want to buy from me in case the taint of silence has slipped into my fragrances.

Instead she stays in the house and cooks and cleans. I come home and the house reeks with the scent of balms she rubs into bruises from moving around the unfamiliar rooms. Yet I cannot deny she cares for me well and shows interest in my work. I start bringing bottles of essence home and teaching them to her. Help her learn sandalwood from saffron and rosemary from rosehip. Though my tolerance for her in my life grows I still cannot bear for that unmarked skin to touch me and flinch away when her hand goes to rest on my arm.

I smell tears as I walk in, a slight tang in the cold air of the house. It takes time to find her, curled up by the side of the bed. I ask what is wrong. She says nothing. Without thinking, without giving my revulsion time to overrule my instinct, I hold her hand, stroking the back of her fingers. I lean in and kiss her cheek. She still does not move, but her back is less tense. At a loss how else to help I go into the kitchen and prepare a meal for her. I do not know what to say to take the sadness away, so instead I steam fish and mushrooms and pour a small glass of wine before leading her to the table. Still she says nothing. I place the fork in her hand, spear the scales of the fish and bring it up to her mouth. Still she says nothing, but when my hand brushes her face her cheeks are dry and I am sure she is smiling.

"It's been a while since I've prepared food," I say. "Have I removed all the bones?"

"There are no bones, but something is missing."

My heart sinks.

"The fish is a bit dry," she says. "It needs butter."

I go to the cupboard and bring the butter to the table, cutting off a slice and letting it settle on her fish. I hear her chew, then she pauses.

"Has the butter made it more palatable?" I ask.

"There is still something not quite right," she says. "This butter is unsalted. It needs a little salt."

"But I have no salt here," I say, disappointed to have let her down.

"Reach under your bed and get your old clothes."

I climb up, groping around for the shirt and trousers. Amongst the mud I find a little salt. When I come back to the kitchen she is melting butter, and I crumble in the crystals. I hear her dip in a spoon and taste the butter, then sigh.

"What's wrong?" I ask.

"There is still something missing," she says.

I wait for her to speak again. I want her to enjoy this meal. She deserves some happiness, I think to myself.

"A pinch or two of wild garlic would make it perfect."

"I don't keep garlic," I say.

"Surely there will be a few leaves stuck in the folds of your clothes."

I find the garments on the floor. The leaves are old yet still pungent, enough to stain my fingers. I find three and take them across to where she tends the pan, break them into pieces and drop them into the now salty butter.

As the cooking stones warm, the acrid mixture rises around us sticking to our face and hair. I stand behind her and put my arms around her waist.

Her fingertips change first, calluses erupting through the skin. She is a musician, left handed and her touch knows the caress of strings, shaping the air itself. Veins rise in her hand, thick and strong. I place my hand against her cheek, slick with condensation. Marks put there by the inscriber's chisel spread. Each one rises like the scent of leaves crushed between mortar and pestle, and as with the most aromatic of herbs my breath catches in my throat. The branches on her forehead are many, but less than mine. I find the scar of where she grew up, and the journeys she made to come to the market, what her trade is and how many honours she has been awarded. I want to tell her how beautiful she is, but words evade me. All I can hear is her breathing. All I can taste is her breath tinged with honeysuckle and jasmine. Lines appear around her eyes like footprints in clay. They tell me more of her life has been spent laughing than crying, though there is deep sorrow held on her face too. On her left cheek three marks for children born, on her right two for those who did not survive. My touch explores her face and the reality of my cruelty is laid before me. It is her turn to kiss away my tears. I find my tongue and speak quiet apologies. She kisses these away too.

Later, when she sleeps, I wipe the perfume from behind ears.

Ours is a marriage of things not said and things not asked, but I am not a young man and I am content, and though it is one of the things never said or asked I think she is content too.

STEVE TOASE lives in North Yorkshire, England and occasionally Munich, Germany. His stories tend towards the unsettling and unreal, dealing with revenge, loss, faery, chess playing bears and ancient gods. In his writing Steve explores the places where other worlds seep into ours.

"I first encountered the concept of the loathly lady many years ago in the story of Niall NaoiGhiallach and Sovereignty. What struck me, reading with modern eyes, was the subtext of looking beyond the surface and overcoming prejudices.

When I saw the theme for this issue I knew I wanted to attempt to write a story, but approach it from a slightly different angle.

In western society the vast majority of concepts of beauty are based on the visual. So I started to think about how beauty would be expressed in a world with no light. By setting 'Skin Like Carapace' in a world where light is absent I could explore how beauty might be expressed in touch, scent and sound. For example instead of child-like smooth skin being the height of attractiveness wrinkles and scars are desirable.

One of the hardest parts of writing 'Skin Like Carapace' was having to ensure there were no visual metaphors in the text as these would be alien in the Land of No Light.

Hopefully this brings a slightly different approach to an ancient and important story."

SOVEREIGNTY: A PROLOGUE
Sara Cleto

BEAUTY BORED ME.

The gowns, the jewels, all the paraphernalia accumulated by young and coveted ladies have a strangely wearying effect, as if the belle in question must constantly carry her worldly spoils on her immaculate shoulders. I trembled beneath the weight.

Men and women leered at me, their ravenous eyes narrowing as they parsed my body into pieces that would never tally to the original sum. I was cherry lips, raven hair, starry eyes—an accumulation of exquisite, ornamental parts. I longed to speak with an unguarded tongue, to dance wildly in a storm of my unbound hair, to go where I willed, when I desired, without restraint or qualification. My mounting wishes parched my lips and clouded my eyes.

Husk-dry and half-blind, I stole into the forest.

Roots boiled mutinously through the path until my slippers fell from my feet, and the branches shredded my shawl and gown. I wiggled my toes into the cool, wet dirt and raised my arms so that my tattered sleeves were luminous wings, and I laughed, wildly, joyfully. The roots and branches recognized my voice and drew respectfully away from me to reveal a clearing.

In the center of the clearing waited a small, thatched house.

The door swung open, and the witch welcomed me to her fireside, offering me a steaming cup. Her long black hair tumbled past her knees in tangled curls, and in her eyes I saw myself reflected whole. She asked me the name of my heart's desire. My fingers curled around the cup, and I told her about the boredom, the weight, the gradual attrition of my existence that occurred when eyes chipped ruthlessly, ceaselessly into me.

She grinned at me, her mouth full of teeth. "Sovereignty. What you want is sovereignty."

The witch bade me drink from my cup, and when I met her eyes, my reflection had changed. My lips grimaced, my hair hung lank and dull, and my body bulged and twisted in unseemly abandon.

Hideous. Abject. Loathly.

But my limbs felt strong, and my voice rang deeper, louder. I laughed again, and clinked my glass against the witch's.

I roamed the woods and danced under the moon and in the darkness of its absence. I climbed trees and threw acorns at passing woodsmen who found my antics baffling but would still converse with me as a person rather than a collection of lovely bits. I ate and slept and sang my fill, until I was truly my own master and sovereignty nestled into my bones.

Though my new reflection pleased me, I always knew I would one day reclaim my own lips and hair and eyes. Not because they were desirable, flawless ornaments but because they were mine. I longed to feel sovereignty fill my own body like dark wine.

One day I spied a knight from my lofty perch. He wore the glazed, stupid-cruel look so common to courtiers, but a mounting desperation had begun to fracture his careful facade.

Who would he be when it shattered?

Curious, I dropped from my branch to land lightly at his feet. He recoiled only slightly from my borrowed visage, concealing his reaction with a flourishing bow.

"Please, good mother, if you can tell me what it is that women most desire, I shall bestow upon you whatever you will, within my power."

He was ripe for me. I extended my gnarled hand, and he grasped it.

SARA CLETO is currently pursuing her PhD in English at the Ohio State University. She is obsessed with fairy tales, coffee, and obtaining more stamps on her passport. Her work can be found or is forthcoming in *Cabinet des Fées, Mirror Dance, Eternal Haunted Summer,* and *Niteblade.*

"Beauty is captivating but often very insidious, and I'm certainly not immune to it. But I have always been invested in complicating its definition and pushing against its limits. Conventional beauty can be constraining, and a Loathly Lady has access to certain freedoms that a lovely princess almost never achieves. I began writing with the question *What happens when a princess simply can't stand being a beautiful object anymore?* and went where it took me."

OLD OAK & THE MAIDEN

A.L. Loveday

THE SUN WAS LOW IN THE SKY, AND THE DESCENDING RAYS BOUNCED off the copper hair of a young woman making her away across the dry fields, surrounding her with a halo of blazing fire. The last of the bird song overlapped with the chirruping of the first chorus of night-insects, and the smell of warm grass was tinged at the edges with the dark, musky scent of approaching darkness.

She wore a long white dress that trailed behind her on the ground; grass and mud stained the hem as she pounded it repetitively into the earth with her calloused bare feet.

A single tear trailed down her cheek.

As the sun finally sank beyond the horizon, the maiden found herself at the edge of a vast and ancient forest. She stopped. Her village was far behind her—she had been walking for hours. A thick wall of knotted wood and twisted vines faced her, daring her to go further, to ignore their menacing barrier.

She hesitated a moment, then stepped forward determinedly, barely flinching as small stones and sharp twigs pierced the flesh on the soles of her feet. She wound her way through entwined branches, ducked under low-hanging fans of leaves, and scrambled over thick roots that rose high above the soil, her skirts hitched clumsily above her knees. Despite the obstacles, she maintained a distinct air of grace and gentility.

Moonlight began to drip through the treetops, and speckled silver lit her way. The glow enhanced her pale face and made her blue eyes flash grey. She moved so smoothly and assuredly over the rough terrain that she could have been mistaken for a ghost.

At the very heart of the forest, where no stars could be seen through the treetops, where no animals dwelled and where silence was as thick as honey, she stopped. She had arrived before an ancient oak tree, and mustering the final dregs of her energy she curtseyed in front of the thick, gnarled bark, before collapsing onto the floor and relinquishing into sobs. She had shed the last of her grace.

Time expanded and contracted, and moved in the mysterious patterns called forth by solitude. She didn't know how long she stayed curled up amongst the dead leaves and her dirty dress, but enough time had elapsed for her to fall quiet once more.

The tree spoke to her at last.

'Fair maiden, you did not come all this way to simply cry at my roots. Tell me your troubles.'

The voice was old and hoarse, as scratchy as bark and as deep as its far-reaching roots. The girl looked up into the labyrinthine grooves and dark knots of the wise old tree, and knew she could be honest. Any fear she held dissipated into the night.

'I need advice,' she murmured, her voice threatening to break, 'the man I love does not notice me because I am not as pretty as the other women in the village. I would give him my heart if only he would let me. I would care for him if he fell ill, work night and day if we grew poor, and give up my life if it would spare his!'

As her confidence grew, so too did her voice, until it was almost a shout. The tree ruffled its leaves in indignation at the disruption of its peace, and the follies of first love.

'What would you have me give you to fulfil your heart's desire?'

'Well,' said the girl, wiping her eyes and smudging dirt on her cheeks, 'I would have you give me a way to become more beautiful than all the other women who steal his gaze. There is no other way...' she choked back a despairing sob.

The tree shook the branch closest to the maiden, and unfurled a new shoot to reveal a bright red bud.

'Take this fruit and dry it for one lunar cycle, then open the skin and you will find a handful of magic seeds. Put one seed in the food of the woman who distracts your true love, and overnight her skin will burn, blister and burst—the fires of your pain will ravage her until she loses all the lustre in her eyes. The man you desire will fall into your arms without question.'

The girl, whose hand had been hovering over the ripe fruit, gasped and drew back slightly. Then, slowly, she moved as if to pluck the fruit off its stalk, but at the last second snatched her hand away again.

'I cannot do it!' she cried, fresh tears welling up in her eyes, 'My love for him would be tainted should I gain his affection by this method... I cannot believe... I... I considered...' her words faded away as she fought back violent cries.

'No... no thank you,' she managed to splutter, and with an awkward curtsey she turned and fled from the sacred grove.

The Old Oak simply drew back its offering, and watched as she disappeared into the undergrowth.

She ran all the way home in the dark, tearing through thorny shrubs and straggling branches, tripping over roots and tearing the soles of her feet to shreds before she emerged onto open fields once more, and could run light footed with home now visible in the distance, bathed in moonlight.

As she walked through the streets and lanes her tears left gleaming trails, like stardust, along her face. They formed an intricate network, a spider's web of lace.

The soft sounds of her crying roused one man from his sleep—as he stepped outside to find out who was responsible for this strange noise at such a late hour, the girl's heart leapt into her throat.

'Why are you crying?' he asked, mesmerised by the diamond sparkle of the tears in her eyes.

Because I was nearly tempted into a sinful deal for love of you, she wanted to say. Instead she shook her head and continued to cry, wherefore the man, now besotted with this weeping beauty, strode forward and enveloped her in his warm arms.

'Do not be sad,' he whispered kindly, kissing her tangled, coppery hair, 'I will keep you safe.'

॒

THE SUN BEAT DOWN HOTLY ON THE WOMAN'S BACK. SHE STRODE forward assuredly, but occasionally looked back over her shoulder as if she feared being followed. Untying her pinafore, she stowed it beneath a young hawthorn bush, not wanting to dirty the clean linen; she clearly remembered soiling her garments during the trip she had made many years before.

She tugged uncomfortably at the collar of her dress as she trudged through the fields, finding the journey tired her more easily now that the gifts of youth had faded away. Sweat began to trickle over her tanned skin, marked faintly with creases and lines, and her coppery hair, now streaked with the first strands of grey, stuck to the back of her neck.

As she approached the entrance to the woods she bit her lip, fearing she would not remember the way.

No, she told herself, the sacred grove can always be found by those who seek it.

As the trees closed in around her the humidity stuck to her skin with the consistency of treacle, and with the persistency of burrs. No matter how she fanned herself or loosened her clothes, she could do nothing to ease her muggy discomfort. The humid scent of warm, damp moss was the only thing she could smell, and as she gulped in unsatisfying mouthfuls of warm, heavy air, she reminded herself why she was making such a hellish journey.

Setting her jaw, she continued forward into the darkening woods and walked until her feet ached and her chest was constricting itself, fighting bitterly for fresh air.

It was with great relief that she entered the clearing once more, and found herself in an eerie darkness and closeness that was both familiar and alien. She made her curtsey to the Old Oak tree, then fell to her knees on the spot. She was without energy even to stand up straight.

It didn't startle her when she heard the creak and rustle of bark stretching, and she didn't jump when she felt the branches prodding at her doughy flesh or pulling at her thinning hair. A soft green leaf traced the lines spreading from the corners of her eyes, before breaking free of its branch and floating lazily into her lap.

The woman looked up into the knotted face of the Oak.

'I need more advice,' she stated, '...if you will give it to me again.'

'I am listening,' said the wise Old Oak.

The woman took a deep breath and began to tell the tree of her problems: 'My husband and I work hard to provide for our children, yet we can barely put enough food on the table, or decent clothes on their backs—' she paused, letting bitter feelings run a course though her veins, indulging in a rare moment in which she allowed herself to feel ugly emotions. 'It pains me to see the way they look at others, with longing and jealousy. They don't understand why... why things aren't *easier* for them. I can accept the hand I have been dealt, but... they're just children. They don't understand. And it isn't fair on them...' she trailed off, and tried not to think about how pitiful she sounded. Despite it all, her children had never openly lamented, but this made it all the harder to bear: they were resigned to their misery.

'What would you have me bestow upon you?'

'I don't know...' she sighed, and thought for a moment, 'I suppose I just wish they could have some of the luxuries that others can afford, simple things: clothes that fit, a decent education, nice food and toys. I want their youth to be a happy time, and I don't want them to grow up feeling resentful and let down.'

The Oak rustled its leaves as it thought about this request. After several long minutes, in which the woman caught her breath relaxed her tired muscles, the tree spoke:

'Look beneath my crooked roots and you will find an ancient stone of great power. Leave it as an offering at the river bed tonight, as the moon rises, and in the morning you shall wake to find the village flooded, and all of your neighbour's most desirable possessions will have been carried by the waters to your home—yours for the taking.'

The woman scrabbled beneath the tree's roots, clawing the damp earth and insects away with her hands until her nails scraped against something rough and hard. She carefully pulled the stone out of the ground and examined it. There were intricate carvings and scriptures in the language of the Other World covering the entire surface, which was no bigger than her fist.

The woman tested the weight of the stone—it would be light enough for her to carry home easily enough, without growing too weary on the journey. Her fingers tingled with excitement, but her heart felt no joy; she should have remembered that the price for the Oak's gifts was often too great.

With a sigh, she replaced the stone into the crudely dug hole and brushed a layer of soil back over the top.

'I cannot do it,' she said sadly, 'How could I look my neighbours in the eye knowing I had robbed them for selfish means? My children may not have beautiful things, but they have beautiful hearts. I fear that I would cause more damage to their souls if they were to have all that they want through deceit and the suffering of others...'

She climbed unsteadily to her feet, taking in a deep lungful of the thick air.

'Thank you, but no.' and with an awkward curtsey she turned and walked away, leaving the Old Oak rustling its leaves in wonder and mirth.

She returned home with her head down, thinking fretfully about what she could possibly do for her family, now that she had walked away from what she believed to be her last resort. She fought the urge to cry, but as she grew closer to the village, and as the darkness encroached, she could not help but allow her tears to fall. She fought back the sobs and cried quietly.

As she passed her neighbour's home, however, the door opened and the wife stepped out, sweeping the steps. She looked up and saw the woman, trudging wearily, crying.

'Oh, what is wrong?' she cried, and rushed to the woman's side. The woman sniffed, and brushed the tears off her pink cheeks and pulled her coppery hair back from her face. She told her neighbour of her fears for her children's happiness, and her pain at not being able to provide for them as she should.

Her neighbour put her arm around her shoulder, 'Don't you worry about them,' she said, 'If there is anything you need, anything at all, I will do what I can for you. We are neighbours, and friends, after all.'

The woman was shocked, and after her having her protests waved away accepted humbly, but began to cry once more out of gratitude to her kind friend, and from guilt, thinking about the offer she was so sorely tempted to accept that would have ruined her. She then thought of her children's smiles, and managed to smile herself through her tears.

THE AWKWARD RHYTHM OF THREE LIMBS UNSTEADILY FIGHTING through the undergrowth could be heard reverberating throughout the forest. Insects took a wide birth around the old woman with the cane, who was hunched forwards and breathing raggedly. She was not old enough to have lost all her flaming hair—although white was by far the most prominent colour—but tragedy and a life of hard work caused her to suffer daily.

Despite the heat she had a shawl wrapped around her shoulders, as these days she grew cold much faster when the sun began it's descent into the west.

She could no longer hear the tread of the wild animals nor the creaking of the boughs over the sound of her own clumsy progression. She had known this would be the case, and tried not to feel too sorry for herself.

She had left soon after breakfast, closed the door to her empty cottage, waved goodbye to her chicken pecking in the yard, and began the long journey that she knew would take the best part of the day.

She smiled with relief as she felt the air close in around her, and saw the light begin to appear in smaller and smaller patches through the canopy.

'Now, which one is it?' she thought to herself, looking around at the ancient trees that for the first time all appeared the same to her.

As if in answer, a slow, warm gust of wind blew past, and began to dance with the leaves of the ancient oak she had twice before visited.

She turned around and made her way towards it.

'Well, believe it or not, I have come again.'

There was no reply. The woman stood waiting, gradually noticing all the bits of her that ached now that she had stopped moving.

'I... don't know whether you'll be able to help me with this one.'

Still no reply. Wincing, she made sure her cane was firmly on the ground and lowered herself slowly into a sitting position. The earth felt hard and unyielding beneath her brittle bones, and she remembered with a sudden burst of nostalgia how at home she had felt here on her first visit, as if her body and her breathing and everything connected to her were also connected to one living aspect of the forest.

She had been selfish and naive then, yes. But she had been strong and done the right thing. Hadn't she?

She waited and waited, drawing her shawl around her body to prevent the cold from enveloping her bones. She might have dozed for a moment, still leaning on her cane, for she was jerked rudely back into consciousness as it slipped under her weight and went skidding along the ground, lodging itself in the tree.

'Oh, I'm so sorry!' the woman cried out, her voice croaking. She wiggled the stick backwards and forwards and side to side and began to perspire from the effort of it. At last it came free, and as it flew out of the tree and out of her hands, a small, carved stone rolled after it, disturbed from its slumber after many years.

'This again,' the woman said to herself, and with a gentle flick of her wrist rolled it back to where it had come from.

She had been selfish and desperate the last time she had come to visit, and had been aware of it at the time. But she had been strong and done the right thing. Hadn't she?

'I thought I would see you again,' came the deep, rough voice of the Old Oak. Calm washed over the woman after the initial shock of its sudden speech, which had caused her to raise her hand to her heart in alarm.

'Tell me what has come to pass.'

She readjusted her shawl, then looked sadly down at the lines and liver spots that, over the years, had made a home for themselves on her hands.

'The first time I visited you I was just a girl, hopelessly in love. You offered to fix my broken heart in a way that would have caused unimaginable suffering to another, and I could not accept. Yet...I still won the man I loved, who became my husband.'

'I remember this all clearly,' the tree acknowledged, its leaves rustling in encouragement to continue.

'I loved my husband every day and every night. I bore his children and worked hard for our family. But then, one day, a woman he used to desire returned to the village. She had not taken a husband, never had children, and had never worked a hard day in her life. She looked as she did all those years ago, and my husband could resist her no longer. He left me for her on the same day of her return.'

'But this is not the only concern that clouds your heart,' the oak observed as the woman paused to collect herself. A tear fell slowly down her powdery cheek, and with a sniff she continued:

'The last time I visited you I was beginning my journey as a mother, devoted to my children and wanting only the best for them. You offered to provide for them in a way that would have caused unimaginable suffering to another family and I could not accept. Yet... my children still had all their needs and wants fulfilled by the generosity of a friend.'

'I remember all this clearly,' the tree acknowledged, its roots stretching in anticipation of the outcome of these events.

'I believe my children loved me... yes, I'm sure they did. But they saw that my life of hard work was not providing them with what they wanted, and they grew wanting much more. So, shunning hard work and even the idea of love, they left home and travelled to the city for the sole purpose of marrying advantageously in order to have all their desires fulfilled without having to truly earn them.'

'You are troubled by these events that have come to pass and feel it is your own doing,' the Oak stated sombrely, and the woman nodded with tears welling up in her eyes once more.

'I thought I was doing the right thing!' she cried, 'I thought that by accepting your magic I would be inviting disaster to strike in the future, as punishment for the cruelty I had shown. But...disaster has come to pass never the less.'

'And yet you make this journey to me once again.'

The woman nodded, 'I felt it was necessary. I need to find peace of mind and this is the only place I thought I would find it.'

'You wish to quiet the questioning part of your mind that wonders whether things would have been better had you simply accepted my help.'

The woman thought about this for a second.

'No,' she said decisively, 'I don't think I'd like to know.'

The Oak's branches swayed in surprise.

'But I did come here to find peace. Tell me, Great Oak, how have you grown to be so clever?'

'By taking all the knowledge in the world,' the tree replied.

'And how have you grown so wise?'

The tree laughed, which was a beautiful and ancient sound: 'That is a secret.'

'Then, with your knowledge and wisdom you must know what I now want. And this time, I promise I will accept your offer.'

'Head back the way you came and it shall be yours.'

The woman took one last look into the knots and gnarls of the old tree and whispered, 'Thank you.'

She rose, turned and carefully began to pick her way through the bushes and fallen leaves, away from the clearing. Branches reached towards her in welcome, stroking her skin and snagging her skirts. The pools of light began to break through, and the woman saw pollen glinting like diamonds in the patchwork columns of sunlight.

Her footsteps grew heavier and the grip on her stick became unchangeable. Breathing was a laborious task and her lungs felt like lead. She could feel true peace not far away, and with her last strength stepped into one of the columns of light that burst through the treetops.

No sooner had she done so when the tree's magic took full effect, and the woman turned into stone. Unfeeling, still, and in a place where she felt at home, where she would stay for all eternity.

OVER THE YEARS MANY PEOPLE MADE THE PILGRIMAGE TO THE OLD Oak, seeking its advice and its magic, believing it to be Merlin, eternally bound, or even the Green Man himself. As they drew nearer they found the statue of the old woman standing before the entrance to the sacred clearing; they saw her body bent from years of suffering, her walking stick showing her strength to continue, and her hand outstretched in the effort to leave. It was her face that caused the travellers to stare. She looked serene with the smile of approaching tranquillity frozen on her lips, and a single tear of gratitude just spilling out of the corner of her eye.

Some saw her as a welcome. Others, as a warning. And for all, the weight of their decisions and the power of the magic that awaited them became crystal clear.

A.L. LOVEDAY is a part-time student and rest-of-the-time writer living in Brighton, UK. She is inspired by folk and fairy tales and the wonders of the natural world, and her short stories have appeared in *Inkspill*, *Volume*, and *Mirror Dance*. You can find her at http://alloveday.blogspot.co.uk/

"The Loathly Lady figure is commonly associated with medieval romance literature, but in my mind she is also a character from a fairy tale. Her story involves enchantment, promises, escape clauses and transformation, all of which are common themes within the genre. But her curse wasn't broken by a kiss from Prince Charming. Rather, when the Loathly Lady owned the power to make her own choices, *this* is what gave her freedom. And this is the aspect of her story that I wanted to examine: the power of choice, and the empowerment of women who make choices."

Fat Is Not A Fairy Tale

Jane Yolen

I am thinking of a fairy tale,
Cinder Elephant,
Sleeping Tubby,
Snow Weight,
where the princess is not
anorexic, wasp-waisted,
flinging herself down the stairs.

I am thinking of a fairy tale,
Hansel and Great
Repoundsel,
Bounty and the Beast,
where the beauty
has a pillowed breast,
and fingers plump as sausage.

I am thinking of a fairy tale
that is not yet written,
for a teller not yet born,
for a listener not yet conceived,
for a world not yet won,
where everything round is good:
the sun, wheels, cookies, and the princess.

JANE YOLEN, often called "the Hans Christian Andersen of America" (Newsweek) and the "Aesop of the Twentieth Century" (N.Y. Times) is the author of well over 335 books, including OWL MOON, THE DEVIL'S ARITHMETIC, and HOW DO DINOSAURS SAY GOODNIGHT. Her work ranges from children's picture books through middle grade fiction, poetry collections, nonfiction, to novels and poetry and story collections for young adults and adults.

Her books and stories have won an assortment of awards—two Nebulas, a World Fantasy Award, a Caldecott, the Golden Kite Award, three Mythopoeic awards, two Christopher Medals, a nomination for the National Book Award, and the Jewish Book Award, among many others. Her poetry has been nominated three times for the Pushcart Prize. She is also the winner (for body of work) of the World Fantasy Assn. Lifetime Achievement Award, Science Fiction Poetry Association Grand Master Award, the Catholic Library's Regina Medal, the Kerlan Medal from the University of Minnesota, the 2012 du Grummond Medal, the Smith College Alumnae Medal. Six colleges and universities have given her honorary doctorates. Her Skylark Award—given by NESFA, the New England Science Fiction Association—set her good coat on fire. If you need to know more about her, visit her website at: www.janeyolen.com

THE LOATHLY LADY AS MYSTAGOGUE
John Patrick Pazdziora

THE STORY BEGINS, THE WAY MANY DO, WITH A MOTHER. THE MOTHER is arguing with her teenage daughter for not doing her share of the housework. It's when a queen pulls up in a coach and asks what all the shouting is about that things start getting rather odd.

This story from the Brothers Grimm, 'The Three Spinners' (KHM 14; cp. ATU 501), may not be the most obvious place to begin a discussion of the Loathly Lady motif (Thompson D732). The story seems to fall outside the pale of the usual classification; Thompson details D732 as '[m]an disenchants loathsome woman by embracing her'. The most immediately recognisable appearance of the Loathly Lady is of course in Chaucer, when the Wife of Bath tells her own idiosyncratic version of the tale. And it seems easy enough to see what that version of the story has to say about sex and sexual attraction, and how it influences interaction between the genders. But the Loathly Lady, as a figure in folklore and fairy tale, should not be reduced simply to a metonym for gender relations. And there is, I think, an overlapping narrative function of the Loathly Ladies in both KHM 14 and D732; the question is less the disenchantment of the 'loathsome woman', and more the role she plays in the initiatory passage of the protagonist into maturity.

Aging, after all, and the fear of aging, is not simply a matter of changing sexual drive, no matter what Hollywood tells us. Aging turns one's self into the other—first by the growing disparity between the image of one's self held in the mind, and that seen in the mirror. But, secondly and more insidiously, by distancing the aged self of the present from the youthful self of the past. We forget too easily what we were like when we were young, or what it's like to be a child. The challenge is, then, not to project our own misbegotten nostalgia on other children and young people, but to reconcile with, and understand, the other that is our self.

The Loathly Lady, then, stands in folk literature as a question and a warning. She represents the person we will all become eventually, the person we've seen our parents become, the person always present in every society, sometimes revered and sometimes despised. And she asks us not only how society treats the outcast and the aged, but how we treat ourselves.

Spinning

THIS BRINGS US BACK TO THE QUEEN IN THE COACH. THE MOTHER tells the queen that she's shouting because her teenage daughter loves to work so much (she doesn't) that she's been spinning all day (she hasn't) and there's just too much spun flax now to know what to do with (there isn't). Oh, says the queen, I could do with a girl like that, and pays the mother in gold to take the allegedly-hardworking girl away with her. Like any good employer, the queen locks the girl in a room and says that if she does a month's work in a day, she can marry the Crown Prince, but if she doesn't then she'll be slowly chopped into small bits and fed to the pig.

It seems clear from the outset that KHM14 is about the breakdown of maternity—more precisely, about the breakdown of maternal initiatory tradition. The teenage heroine of the tale has been ostensibly abandoned by her mother, and the mother surrogate—the queen who acquires a daughter through capitalist methods—offers no help or support, only threats. The girl is given no support in passing through her adolescence into adulthood and maturity; she is rather rejected on the basis of normal if unflattering teenage behaviour. In the context of the story, at any rate, she is told by both familial structures, in the form of her mother, and societal structures, in the form of the queen, simply to *become* what is expected; she is not nurtured but berated.

Into this story walks the loathly lady—or, more correctly, three loathly ladies:

When the maiden was alone again, she did not know what to do or where to turn. In her distress she went over to the window and saw three women coming in her direction: the first had a broad flat foot, the second had such a large lower lip that it hung down over her chin. And the third had an immense thumb. They stopped in front of her window, looked up, and asked the maiden what the matter was. (Zipes's translation, p. 69)

The nature of their entry into the tale is significant. By comparison, in *The Wife of Bath's Tale*, the loathly lady appears just after the dishonoured knight has vainly pursued a vision of twenty-four dancing maidens on the green:

No creature saugh he that bar lyf,
Save on the grene he saugh sittynge a wyf—
A fouler wight ther may no man devyse.
Agayn the knyght this olde wyf gan ryse,
And seyde, "Sire knyght, heer forth ne lith no wey.
Tel me what that ye seken, by youre fey!
Paraventure it may the bettre be;
Thise olde folk kan muchel thyng," quod she. (lines 997-1004)

It seems worth noting that when the knight is introduced as 'a lusty bacheler' (line 883), and seems to have been rather popular with the ladies (lines 894-900); yet this self-confidence is shown to be ultimately destructive when he commits a crime of passion, sexually assaulting a young woman, and finds himself facing a death sentence (lines 879-893). He is spared only if he can to find—in a clear burlesque of a typical quest of Medieval romance—'[w]hat thyng is it that wommen moost desiren' (line 905); the implication is that whatever it is, it certainly isn't him or his sexual attentions. But on the course of his quest,

he ne koude arryven in no coost
Wher as he myghte fynde in this mateere
Two creatures accordynge in-feere. (lines 922-924)

Curiously, the knight, not unlike the lazy girl in KHM 14, has been
abandoned on the cusp of his initiation into adulthood, intellectually if
not physically. His life quite literally depends on being able to empathise
with the needs of women, and the abandonment of his selfish adolescent
passion, in much the way the lazy girl must overcome her adolescent
laziness. The nature of their offenses is, of course, as different as the
historical epochs and ideologies of Chaucer and the Grimms; nor is
it necessary to suggest that the Grimms were influenced by Chaucer.
The similarity appears to emerge, rather, with the use of the motif of
the loathly lady: the young protagonist, facing death because of their
inability to transition from adolescence to adulthood, finds themselves
in a liminal space, neither child nor adult. In the knight's case, this
is signified by the quest leading him 'under a forest syde' and into a
fairy ring (line 899-996, cf. lines 857-864); in the lazy girl's case, it is
indicated through the unlikely adoption by the queen. Each has been
exiled from society and given over to the magical realm; neither is
capable of redeeming themselves on their own. It is in this crisis that
the loathly lady appears. She is herself liminal in that she occupies a
similar transitional state; her extreme advanced age suggests that she
occupies the space between life and death—perhaps, curiously, as
close to death as the young person she takes in charge. And she takes
upon herself responsibility to teach the vulnerable and abandoned
young person the knowledge they are being punished for not having;
she facilitates the initiation and relays the accumulated wisdom of
the inherited tradition with her cunning remark: 'Thise olde folk kan
muchel thyng' (line 1004).

In the knight's case, the loathly lady gives him a rather
straightforward, more than a little bawdy lesson in gender relationships
and knightly conduct; here the thumbprints of the literary rewriter are
in evidence. But in 'The Three Spinners', the lesson of the loathly ladies

is more polyvalent, tied more directly into the use of folklore in general and the loathly lady motif in particular. The three spinning women sit and spin the thread for the girl. This is, indeed, fairy tale pedagogy, but not in the way that we as modern readers might perhaps prefer it. The three old women do not teach the girl to take care of herself, or overcome her laziness; they don't even give her a lecture on accepting herself and being happy with who she is. Rather, they complete the whole of her spinning: they give her, not the resources to create her own story, but the whole of the inherited narrative tradition of story. She is given an established order for her to find her place in; she does not need to create her own story because the tradition of the folk is there. Thus in initiating the girl into womanhood, out of childhood into full maturity, the loathly ladies take upon themselves the primary role that the mother and the queen both lacked: that of passing on the tradition to the girl.

This is an important distinction; the loathly lady has a different function in the folkloric tradition than that of the magical helper, as popularized by Joseph Campbell's discussion of the Spider Woman (p. 69ff). She is, rather, a mystagogue, overseeing and guiding the protagonist's ritual passage through seemingly impossible tasks into her matrilineal tradition. Recall that when the 'olde wyf' secures the success of the knight's quest, she does not simply point the way he should go; she teaches him the whole of the answer he needs (line 1050). She does not give him the means to answer the question himself, but rather entrusts to him, intact, the wisdom she already possess— though whether she has acquired it magically or simply from her own long experience is not entirely clear.

MINING

THE ROLE OF THE LOATHLY LADY AS A TRANSMITTER OF TRADITION appears again in another curious iteration of the motif, *The Princess and Curdie* (1884) by the Scottish author George MacDonald. This children's novel was written as follow-up for his earlier book *The Princess and the Goblin* (1872), and focuses chiefly on the character of the miner boy, Curdie, who had helped stave off a goblin invasion in the previous book. As that might suggest, the world of MacDonald's *Princess* books is steeped in Scottish folklore. When fantastic experiences begin to happen to Curdie, particularly his encounter with the beautiful and cryptic Lady of the Silver Moon and her spinning wheel—a being he has heard of but not before encountered—the narrative quickly begins to frame them within the folkloric tradition. His mother, first, tells him about her own encounter with the Lady of the Silver Moon, and, second, as he is working in the mine the next day the other miners begin telling folktales. The narrator makes it clear that the stories they are relating are part of the tradition handed down matrilineally:

> Their wives and mothers and grandmothers were their chief authorities. For when they sat by their firesides they heard their wives telling their children the selfsame tales, with little differences, and here and there one they had not heard before, which they had heard their mothers and grandmothers tell in one or other of the same cottages. (p. 39)

The stories the miners tell concern someone they call 'a witch, an old hating witch, whose delight was to do mischief' (p. 40). The passage is curious, and worth quoting at some length:

> At length they came to speak of a certain strange being they called Old Mother Wotherwop. Some said their wives had seen her. It appeared as they talked that not one had seen her more than once. Some of their mothers and grandmothers, however, had seen her also, and they all had told them tales about her when they were children. They said that she could take any shape she liked, but that in reality she was a withered old woman, so old and so withered that she was as thin as a sieve with a lamp behind it; and that she was never seen except at night, and when something terrible had taken

place, or was going to take place—such as the falling in of the
roof of a mine, or the breaking out of water in it. (pp. 39-40)

I have so far been unable to identify a direct folkloric source for this
tale; it seems likely that, unless it stems from an unrecorded oral
tradition, MacDonald created Old Mother Wotherwop out of his own
imagination. If so, it is a remarkably convincing bit of 'fakelore', as
it were; in the world of the story, at any rate, it is genuinely folkloric,
almost believed by the miners, for all their laughter at the telling. They
attribute any number of their misfortunes to her malevolence: sour
wells, a tumble into a bog while drunk, the death of a cow, gatherings
of goblins (pp. 40, 42). The influence of this loathly lady is agreed to be
negative, because, they say, 'a woman like that was so much more likely
to be bad than good' (p. 41).

And yet, as MacDonald points out through the laconic commentary
of the miner Peter, Curdie's father, the most troubling aspect of the
miners' story is how readily they agree that an old woman shuffling
around by herself at night must be a sinister being. Her greatest
deception, they say, is when 'she took the shape of a young woman
sometimes, as beautiful as an angel', and struck men blind; this
anecdote prompts Peter to ask 'whether she might not as likely be an
angel that took the form of an old woman, as an old woman that took
the form of an angel' (p. 40). His suggestion meets scoffing dismissal:
'They said an old woman might be very glad to make herself look like
a young one, but who ever heard of a young and beautiful one making
herself look old and ugly?' (pp. 40-41).

This accentuates the most remarkable feature of the loathly lady:
as the knight in Chaucer discovers to his relief, she is indeed 'yong
and fair' (line 1223); she assumes the guise of age in order to teach
the knight a lesson. The loathly aspect of Old Mother Wotherwop, too,
turns out to be one of perception, largely for the purpose of instruction.
When Curdie and his father at last meet the Lady of the Silver Moon
in a majestic underground cavern, she appears as 'a lady, beautiful
exceedingly, dressed in something pale green, like velvet, over which

her hair fell in cataracts of a rich golden colour' (p. 47); the narrator further clarifies that

> all the beauty of the cavern, yes, of all [Curdie] knew of the whole creation, seemed gathered in one centre of harmony and loveliness in the person of the ancient lady who stood before him in the very summer of beauty and strength. (p. 49)

Yet she freely identifies herself as the selfsame Old Mother Wotherwop (p. 53). The true aspect of this loathly lady, then, is not simply a beautiful woman but the female personification of the platonic ideal of Beauty. Her physical appearance metamorphoses in response to the ability of the individual beholder to recognize Beauty in whatever form it takes. In essence she is, as the narrator describes, 'the woman that was old yet young' (p. 53); the tale of the cruel old woman who's just the sort to do spiteful things arises from fear and misunderstanding of Beauty and its place in the world. So she explains: 'Shapes are only dresses, Curdie, and dresses are only names. That which is inside is the same all the time. [...] It is one thing the shape I choose to put on, and quite another the shape that foolish talk and nursery tale may please to put on me' (pp. 55, 56). She fulfils the role of a mystagogue by initiating Curdie— through fire, no less—into the perception of the insides of things, rather than the shape; this knowledge both sustains him through and provides the solution to his subsequent quest.

Welcoming

The loathly lady, then, teaches her lessons through paradox and inversion: she reveals beauty through a guise of ugliness. This, more than spinning and the social and folkloric tradition it suggests, seems to be the lesson of the loathly ladies in 'The Three Spinners'. They spin the flax for the lazy girl, sparing her life and her helping her transition into womanhood, on one condition: 'only if you invite us to your wedding and are not ashamed of us'; this, they say, 'will determine your good fortune' (p. 69). As they have become surrogate mothers for the lazy girl, giving her a passage from childhood to womanhood, so she must be willing to identify with them in spite of and perhaps because of their hideousness. And the girl does, declaring that 'since they have done so many good things for me, I'd like to remember them in my happiness' (p. 70). In her case, it all ends comically, with her new bridegroom being so appalled by the spinning women's loathsome appearances that he bans his wife from ever working again in her life. And 'The Three Spinners' can be truly hilarious when told by a capable storyteller. But the seriousness of the theme remains. The culmination of the lazy girl's initiation into womanhood and marriage is an act of empathy, identification with the marginalized and the outcast; she enters adulthood when she has the courage to welcome the stranger as a friend.

MacDonald draws out this theme specifically in his short story 'Little Daylight' (1869), perhaps one of the most poignant uses of motif D732 in a literary fairy tale. In this story, Princess Daylight is cursed to sleep all day, all night she shall wax and wane with its mistress, the moon' (*Complete*, p. 151). When the moon is full, she takes the form of a beautiful maiden, but when the moon wanes 'she looked, when the moon was small or gone, like an old woman exhausted with suffering' (p. 153) The wandering prince who falls in love with the beautiful Princess Daylight is unaware of the nature of the curse, and when he meets her in the forest as a withered old woman, he responds entirely sympathetically, actually abandoning his quest to find the princess in order to help the old woman (p. 163); his kindness to her breaks the spell and her shape returns to her own youthful beauty. The loathly lady thus shows him the fulfilment of his quest, while being the fulfilment at the same time. In this instance, the prince's empathy seems to be prompted by his own recent sufferings; he is in fact fleeing from revolution and genocide (p. 154). But more significantly, for all his love and adoration of the princess, the prince breaks the enchantment and fulfils his quest only when he turns aside for an act of compassion.

WORKS CITED

Campbell, Jospeh. *The Hero with a Thousand Faces*. London: Fontana, 1993.

Chaucer, Geoffrey. *The Wife of Bath's Tale*. In *The Riverside Chaucer*. Edited by Larry D. Benson. Third Edition. Oxford: Oxford University Press, 2008.

Grimm, Jacob and Wilhelm Grimm. *The Complete Fairy Tales*. Translated by Jack Zipes. Third Edition. London: Vintage Books, 2007.

MacDonald, George. *The Princess and Curdie*. New York: Puffin Books, 1994.

---. *The Complete Fairy Tales*. Edited by U. C. Knoepflmacher. London: Penguin, 1999.

Thompson, Stith. *Motif-index of folk-literature : a classification of narrative elements in folktales, ballads, myths, fables, mediaeval romances, exempla, fabliaux, jest-books, and local legends*. Revised and Enlarged Edition. Bloomington: Indiana University Press, 1955-1958. http://www.ualberta.ca/~urban/Projects/English/Motif_Index.htm.

JOHN PATRICK PAZDZIORA (PGDip, Belfast Bible College) is completing his PhD at the University of St Andrews. His dissertation examines George MacDonald's writings for children in the context of the Scottish literary tradition. He has published articles on various authors, including James Thurber and Andrew Lang. He is the co-editor of *Re-Thinking George MacDonald: Contexts and Contemporaries* (ASLS, 2013) with Christopher MacLachlan and Ginger Stelle, *New Fairy Tales: Essays and Stories* (Unlocking, 2013) with Defne Çizakça, and serves as the general editor of *Unsettling Wonder* (www.unsettlingwonder.com). John lives in Scotland with his family.

SPECIAL THANKS

RIMA STAINES, whose painting "Telling Stories to the Trees" appears on the cover, is an artist using paint, wood, word, music, animation, clock-making, puppetry and story to attempt to build a gate through the hedge between the worlds.

Rima's inspirations include the world of folktale; nomadic living; Old Europe; magics of every feather; wilderness, plant-lore; the margins of thought, community and spirituality; and the beauty in otherness.

Rima lives on the wild edge of Dartmoor, UK with her beloved, Tom, & their big-hearted ice-eyed lurcher Macha. You can join her caravan here: intothehermitage.blogspot.com

 You can also find Rima's work at the following:

www.the-hermitage.org.uk
www.onceuponoclock.com
www.thehermitage.etsy.com

BROOKE SHADEN, whose self-portrait "Wallen" appears on page 41, is a fine art photographer living and working in the Los Angeles area. She began creating self-portraits for ease and to have full control over the images, and has since grown into a self-portrait artist. Self portraiture for her is not autobiographical in nature. Instead, she attempts to place herself within worlds she wishes we could live in, where secrets float out in the open, where the impossible becomes possible. Her vision extends beyond the realm of the camera, creating images that resemble paintings and speak of an era that is not our own. Each image is a story. Visit her website at http://brookeshaden.com.

TO THE ARTISTS

KIRSTY GREENWOOD's "Study of a Gug II" (front) and "Gug Girl" (back) were inspired by H.P Lovrcraft's Gugs, loathly beasts indeed. With the advantage of an illustrative mind-set, Kirsty is motivated by ephemeral visual misunderstanding, transient half-light, ocular strangeness, nightmares, dreams and fleeting glimpses of unreality.

Inspired by faerie tales, myths and legends, ailuroanthropy, science, Alice-syndrome and transformation, childhood memories, ghost stories, naiveté, music, antique cultures, the minds of other artists, Quixotism and true romanticism; her idiosyncratic work often has its roots in dreamlike non-realities to create Art contained by the renovating of influences and ideas into images which often convey feelings of otherworldly states and a desire to know more of the subject.

Favouring pencil and ink, mixing with photography and print, Greenwood likes to work intricately to produce detailed phantasmagorias and unusual scenarios or beings representing the worlds of both traditional and modern stories of all genres.

Kirsty lives in her native North Yorkshire and is heavily influenced by the rural Dales landscape she grew up in, literature, music and Art of all varieties. For further examples or to commission work please visit www.kirstygreenwood.co.uk